CRAVEN'S WAR
THE FINAL CHANCE

NICK S. THOMAS

Copyright © 2023 Nick S. Thomas

All rights reserved.

ISBN: 979-8327132580

PROLOGUE

The campaign of 1812 had started far earlier than anyone could have expected when Wellington ordered an advance on the opening day of the New Year. The army had suffered through snowstorms, hail, freezing temperatures, and wolf-infested lands with limited rations, but the gamble had paid off. The city had been captured in less than two weeks, long before the French armies under Marshal Marmont in Spain could march to relieve the siege.

Yet the success had come at an enormous cost as the dead lined the breaches of the great old fortress city, but Wellington now has a foothold in Spain. Craven, now a Major, has enjoyed successes of his own, even against his old nemesis, Major Bouchard, who he defeated in single combat and sent him fleeing in humiliation.

The melancholy of the winter months has been shrugged off, and the senior officers who once spoke openly about

Wellington's inevitable failure began to believe a great triumph was in sight. Yet a great many obstacles stand between Wellington and any hope of striking into France. The French still remain in control of most of Spain, with the last remaining Spanish armies seemingly unable to put up any degree of resistance, unlike the irregular forces throughout the nation who go on punishing the French at every turn as they fight their guerrilla war.

Ciudad Rodrigo was one of the keys to Spain, but there is another, and it must be overcome if Spain is to be freed from Napoleon's grasp. If Badajoz cannot be overcome, it will be the end of the Peninsula War. For Wellington's army it is the final chance.

CHAPTER 1

23rd January 1812.
Two days had passed since the taking of the fortress of Ciudad Rodrigo, but the air remained thick with ash from the city where several buildings were still burning whilst other structures had been reduced to smouldering ruins. At least the fires went some way to masking the stench of death as the burial of thousands was organised. More than a thousand of which were the soldiers of both sides who had died in the siege. Hundreds of civilians were amongst them, and many more soldiers died of their wounds every day.

Work parties worked all hours to reconstruct the fortifications they had targeted with heavy guns only days before. It was a frenzied rush to restore the city to a defensible state, and that did not give any of the troops a feeling of security, for they knew why the works were so urgent.

"Will Marmont come, Sir?" Paget asked as he approached

to look upon the newly captured city from the same vantage point and house that had been their home for the past weeks.

Craven shrugged as he had no more idea than the Lieutenant.

"A little singlestick to get the blood flowing on this cold morning, Sir?" Paget sounded enthusiastic.

He looked back and noted Hawkshaw had joined them also, and the bleak expression about his face spoke volumes. He had seen far too much of war. Craven shook his head in response to Paget.

"We have done enough fighting."

"I never thought I would hear you say as such, Sir."

"I never thought a lot would happen the way it has, nor that I would be there to witness it."

Hawkshaw nodded in appreciation for his introspection and respect for the grave scenes before their eyes.

"Should we not be training ready for whatever comes next? For when Marshal Marmont marches back here to try and take what we have worked hard to achieve? For he will come, won't he, Sir?"

The threat was posed by the formidable French army under Marshal Marmont, a good friend of Napoleon, and who had fought beside the Emperor at some of his great triumphs. Yet Craven was dismissive and shrugged as if he had little care.

"I wonder if you are well, Sir, that you would not want to cudgel?"

"There has been enough fighting in these past days," replied Hawkshaw.

Craven didn't want to admit it, but he agreed with his sentiment. The experience of the bloody breach at the fortress walls was not a thing any of them would forget lightly. And yet Paget seemed to or was at least good at pretending to have the capacity to do so. The tone was solemn, for the elated scenes of success of the siege had given way to the realisation that there was so much more to come, and the dead were still being buried. On top of it all, the shameless looting of the city by British soldiers had soured the victory for many.

"A terrible thing, isn't it?" Matthys joined them.

There were so many awful things, none of them knew which he could be referring to.

"A siege is an ugly affair, and it always is, unless the defenders surrender, and they should have once the breaches had been made."

"They imagined they could hold them, and they nearly did," admitted Craven as he remembered the terrifying struggle and scramble up a near impossible climb under the weight of constant fire.

"I hear the French expected the fortress to hold out for three to four weeks. I should imagine this will come as quite a shock," replied Hawkshaw.

"I thought it would be like any other battle, but I was wrong." Paget looked to the breach, as it was slowly filled, and the defences reconstructed.

Nobody replied but they all felt it. The concentrated horrific violence was nothing like a fight upon the battlefield. There was no manoeuvring nor cover or any ability to break the enemy and see them flee, only a bitter and bloody toil until the job was done. It was not a sight any of them would ever forget and far worse than any battlefield they had ever fought upon.

A small party of riders approached with Major Spring at

their head, but there was no sense or urgency as they moved at only the walk. The Major looked as solemn as the rest of them, perhaps even more so, which was of concern, seeing as he had not taken part in the assault. Was this merely solidarity? They hoped so. The Major rode up and stopped short of them before slumping a little forward in his saddle. He gave a faint but audible sigh as they waited to hear what he had to say, for they were well acquainted and far past formal greetings, despite the uniforms they all wore.

"Bob Craufurd is dead," he finally declared.

"General Craufurd, Sir?" Paget gasped.

They had seen him fall at the breach, but the prospect of that old warhorse dying seemed beyond any of their imaginations. He was the commander of the Light Division and one of Wellington's most trusted, elite, and experienced officers. He had fought the rear guard action on the retreat to Corunna, and a great many battles before and after it. Yet Craven had spent those days avoiding those in command and shirking any responsibility he might be given; he only knew of the General's exploits from more recent actions.

"A dark day," admitted Hawkshaw as he looked to the breach and thought of the hundreds who had fallen alongside the General, and many more who would yet succumb to their wounds just like him.

"What hope is there for the rest of us?" Paget asked.

"It could have happened to any of us. In fact, it did. You can parry a sword, Lieutenant, but not a musket nor cannon ball," replied Craven.

He tried to shrug it off as nothing, but he knew the loss of the General would have a debilitating effect on the army. Black

Bob, as he was affectionately known, was a hard disciplinarian but a tremendously effective and brave officer who inspired those he commanded; the elite light infantry who had worked as both trail blazers and also an indispensable rear guard during the Army's darkest days.

"General Craufurd will be buried in the breach where he fell, as is most fitting for a man of his sort."

Craven nodded in agreement, but Spring waited as if to expect more.

"It would mean a lot to the men of the Light Division to have you there," Spring finally added.

"Me?" Craven questioned.

"You are a lot like him in so many ways, Major. But most of all you embody the light infantry ingenuity and the fighter's spirit which Bob Craufurd stood for. The Army would do well to see you there today."

Craven never truly knew the man, despite fighting over some of the same ground and their brief encounter at the battle of Bussaco, but as he looked to his closest friends and comrades, he could see he had no choice.

"I'll be there."

Spring nodded in appreciation. "Henry MacKinnon was also killed in that almighty blast." He was referring to another General killed in the bloody siege, "A hard won victory, but there will be many more to come, perhaps worse still, for this was our first step into Spain, and there are many more miles to Paris."

"You think we will make it all the way there, Sir?" Paget asked excitedly.

"Not many believe it, not at home and not even many of

the most senior officers of this army, but I think we have proven them wrong enough times to show we can. Wouldn't you say, Lieutenant?"

"Why yes, Sir!"

Major Spring smiled back as he put on a brave face, but there was a lot weighing down both his mind and his shoulders as he rode away.

"A costly affair this was, Sir." Paget was looking at the fortress they had wrestled from the enemy.

"There will be worse to come," declared Hawkshaw.

"Worse than this?"

"Wellington caught the enemy by surprise by an early start to this campaign. The garrison at Ciudad Rodrigo was stretched thin, and our assault struck quickly before it could be strengthened or relieved, but the element of surprise is gone now. We will face far greater resistance with every step we take," admitted Craven.

"I never imagined victory would come at such a cost," lamented Paget.

"Gather all our officers, non-commissioned as well," ordered Craven.

"Is that appropriate?" Hawkshaw asked.

"Major Spring asked us to be there, and we will. Craufurd never did anything by half measure, and neither will we."

His brother rushed off to carry out the orders as he gathered the funeral party.

"You knew him well, Sir?" Paget asked.

"Not really, but well enough to know he was a good soldier, and what he meant to this army. They will take it badly."

"Yes, I fear it is so. Perhaps this damned war will take all of us yet."

Craven smiled a little as he remembered Paget's enthusiasm to join the fight when he was a fresh-faced young officer, but he refrained from jibing him for it, for it was not the time nor place.

"What will Wellington do now, Sir?"

"He'll fight, whether the enemy come to us, or we go to them. The wheels are moving, and the momentum has begun. There is no stopping it now."

Craven imagined the hard days ahead. He went into the house and gathered up his things. Paget watched in amazement to see him brush off his uniform and smarten himself up as best he could, an honour he did not even bestow on Wellington himself when in the General's presence. Everyone amongst them was cleaning and adjusting their uniform and equipment to present as good an image as possible. It was hardly easy. It had been a harsh winter, and an even harsher journey and battle to take the ground they now occupied. Not even Paget looked entirely presentable, which bothered him greatly, but he knew there was nothing to be done about it. Many of them had powder stains and burns in their uniforms which would not come out, and various patches over the wool of their tunics and greatcoats. Their shakos were badly beaten and malformed, not just from the weather, but where they had used the hats as musket rests, leaving the crowns squashed and scruffy.

They did their best, which was more than most of them would ever bother. For they were fighters and not stay at home parade troops. It was a solemn march to the walls for the funeral, as they walked much the same ground they had advanced over when conducting the assault. It was chewed up and scorched by the torrential bombardments that had led up to that violent night and the deadly scramble which followed.

Craven's ears were still ringing from the almighty blast which had killed many, and Paget was no better off, and yet they knew that had they been a few feet closer to the main blast neither of them would have survived. A great many of the Light Division had gathered for the burial of their commanding officer. Wellington himself watched from the sidelines, paying his respects to one of his most experienced and accomplished officers, a loss he would feel as deeply as any of them, having come to rely on Black Bob.

The arrival of Craven and the other officers of the Salfords was not met with any celebration, but certainly some small nods in appreciation. They took up their position far at the back and barely able to see the proceedings where a number of other ranks of the Light Division had gathered to see the General off in their own way. It was a remarkably quiet scene, the clergymen speaking quietly as they conducted the service.

A rifleman wept beside where Craven had stopped, but he did not think anything less of the man. They all had good reason to shed a tear.

"A fine man the General was," he said to comfort the rifleman.

"Yes, Sir. Did you know him well, Sir?" The rifleman had a strong Irish accent.

"No, I am afraid not. We only ever shared a few words, but I fought beside him at Bussaco."

"Then you were in great company. I am afraid I missed that day, for I had been shot under the knee several weeks earlier."

Craven nodded in agreement as he had suffered more than a few similar wounds himself.

"I am sure we served across many a battlefield together," agreed Craven.

The Irishman agreed and was lost deep in thought before blurting out his memories of the fallen General.

"Black Bob was a robust and prickly sort of fellow. A hard driver but also a fair one. He will be remembered for having a heart as cold as stone, but we in the Light Division knew otherwise."

Craven said nothing but could see the grieving man wanted to go on and so let him.

"I saw the heart of Black Bob with my very own eyes. I once saw him chase one of our very own, a Corporal, who had stolen bread from a Spanish woman. A great crime to steal from the starving people of this country who have already been robbed by the French of their lands and everything else. General Craufurd chased down that man himself and was to have the man reduced to the pay and rank of Private, and one hundred and fifty lashes also.

The General was most unsettled to have to punish one of his own, and that Corporal pleaded with the General. He reminded him of the days they had served together in Buenos Aires, and that the Corporal had shared the last of his water and biscuit with the General when they were prisoners together. The Corporal had only been dealt a single lash when Black Bob called a stop to it. The General paced up and down the square uneasily, muttering words to himself. He wiped his face with his handkerchief, trying to hide the emotion that was so evident to us all in that square. A dead silence followed until our gallant

General recovered a little his noble feeling, when he uttered with a broken and sad voice, 'Why does a brave soldier like you commit these crimes?' And with that he left, for it was too sad a scene for him to witness, for him and the rest of us. Needless to say, the Corporal was restored to his rank and pardoned. He had suffered enough, for the shame and disappointment he had caused Black Bob was worse than the lash. He loved us, and that cannot be said for many in his boots."

Craven was rather moved by the story and wished he had gotten to know the General better.

"What's your name?"

"Costello, Sir."

"Major Craven." He held out his hand in friendship, which confused the Irishman, who would never expect to receive such a gentle and friendly gesture from one so senior to him, and his eyes lit up as if he saw a little of Black Bob in Craven.

"Thank you, Sir," he replied as he shook hands.

"I have no doubt Black Bob would have led you all the way to Paris. Let us not disappoint him, ey?"

"No, Sir," replied Costello as tears streamed down his face.

Six Sergeant Majors had carried the coffin of General Craufurd, and there was not a dry eye amongst the rugged veterans as they lowered him into the grave before the breach of the fortress. Rarely if ever had any of them seen such a melancholy scene, despite all the pageantry of the affair. A salute was soon ordered and musket, rifle, and also cannon fire violently ended the tranquil scene. Craven had not seen such despair in the faces of the other ranks since the loss of John

Moore at Corunna. The ceremony did not last long, and soon enough the formations of soldiers were marched away to return to their cantonments, mostly spread out amongst the local dwellings just as Craven and the Salfords had been.

Major Spring approached Craven and his party who had remained behind.

"Thank you," he declared.

"They are not taking it well," replied Craven.

"Would your men if it were you being put in the ground?"

Paget's face became pale with horror at the mere thought of the idea.

"There will be many more dead and buried like Black Bob, good and bad men alike," added Spring.

"This was no noble affair, not like facing an enemy on the field of battle."

Craven wanted to disagree with Paget, as it seemed an absurd statement, after the devastation they had seen across so many battlefields. Yet deep down some part of him agreed with him. A siege was a bitter and savage affair. The concentration of violence in just a few small places was beyond belief, and unlike the battlefield, there was no way to give ground and concede a little to the enemy. It was all or nothing, which was a reminder how another such event lay in their future.

"Badajoz will be worse," he admitted, remembering the last time they had tried to take the fortress. Two sieges had already failed against the dreaded place.

"Worse, Sir?" Paget croaked.

"Indeed, Mr Paget, for Badajoz is far greater a fortification than this place, and with a garrison much, much larger," replied Major Spring.

"Must it be taken?" Paget sniffled.

"It is the second of two keys to Spain. It is not a question of if it must be taken, only when."

"You did not think wrestling Spain from Napoleon's hands would be easy, did you? After all we have lived to see?" Craven pressed.

"I had hoped the enemy would have been weakened by our efforts."

"Weakened, yes, but we were always fighting an uphill battle. There are many who never thought we would get this far, even staff of this very army and a great many of those back home. We must press on and keep proving them wrong," replied Spring.

"When?" Craven asked.

"Whenever the order is given."

"You do not know, Sir?"

"The winter is still upon us, and we have much to prepare to regather our strength."

"You're a good liar," smiled Craven.

Spring smirked in response.

"Then you do know, Sir?" Paget asked excitedly, as marching on was an appealing prospect, no matter how terrifying the destination.

"It doesn't matter what I know. For Wellington will do and change his plans as he pleases. Just be ready, for you will spearhead any movements we make."

"I don't know if that is the very best or very worst of jobs," replied Craven.

"First pick of what there is to be had, and a chance at the enemy with sword and not cannon? I could not think of a better place for you. Major."

He then rode off.

"What did the Major mean, Sir?" They were watching him leave the solemn scene.

"That we are looking for a fight."

"Aren't we, Sir?"

"It rather depends on what kind of fight," replied Craven sternly as he looked to the breach and was reminded of the scenes of devastation, not wanting to relive them nor wish them on any man.

"What now then, Sir?"

"For now, we have some peaceful days and a warm home. We shall not be so lucky in the weeks and months ahead, and so let us not waste them."

They began to shuffle away, revealing Vicenta who had been watching from behind them throughout without being noticed. She looked deep in thought.

"Are you okay?" Craven asked as the rest left them alone.

"The English, you fight as though it were for your own lands and homes, so bravely."

"It is stubbornness mostly. A stubborn will to go on, and many proved themselves the scum they truly are once they got inside that city," lamented Craven.

But she shrugged it off as if it were nothing.

"Soldiers have been acting that way since long before any of us were born, and on all sides. I wish it were different, but it is not, but at least the English aren't ordered to act in this way and encouraged to do so every day."

Craven was surprised she could be so magnanimous, but then he supposed she had little other choice, for she was choosing the best of a bad bunch in a terrible war.

"I am sorry for all you have had to live through," he replied softly.

"Do you know how many have said that to me? It means nothing."

Craven was stunned and did not know how to reply. She looked furious and had every right to be.

"Saying sorry means nothing, acting to make things better means something, and you have done that since the day I first met you. That means something. It means a great deal."

Craven was relieved, for he had seen her wrathful ways and would not to be in the line of fire.

"I didn't come here to help you people of Portugal and Spain. I came here to make my fortune," he admitted.

"None of us are what we were before all of this began."

"That's not entirely true. I am still poor," he smiled.

"Then take your riches from the French."

He appreciated the sentiment, but as he looked up to the breach and watched the wall be reconstructed, he knew there would be a hard fight to take anything from the hands of the enemy.

CHAPTER 2

Paget and Craven paced along a dirt track encircling the city, stretching their legs on another cold and damp day as they waited on news to depart.

"I don't know what is worse, Sir, the assault or the waiting for something to happen."

"I wouldn't wish that night on any man. Well not any I like with any part of my being," replied Craven sternly.

Paget nodded in agreement as he felt a little foolish for making such a ridiculous comparison. They could see a gathering of troops ahead around a group of mules. It was a noisy crowd as if they were impatiently awaiting some great excitement. At the edge of the crowd, they could see Birback who was near salivating at the sight.

"What is this?" Craven demanded.

"Those muleteers drive a great horde of rum and biscuits through here, and they won't share," he replied without taking his eyes off the mules who were heavily laden with pig skins full of rum, ripe for the taking as he saw it.

The crowd was getting rowdy as a soldier grabbed hold of one muleteer.

"This is going to get ugly, Sir," declared Paget.

Craven did not want to interfere. He rather fancied the treasure for himself just as Birback did, but a pistol shot ignited. It brought them all to silence as a waft of powder smoke swirled about them. The mob turned about to see Major Rooke holding the smoking pistol.

"You will not touch those provisions. Now disperse!"

The Major brought with him a dozen soldiers with muskets in hand to enforce his orders, and so the mob soon left the scene amid sighs and curses of disappointment. The newly arrived soldiers took up positions around the laden mules to protect their valuable cargo. Rooke soon caught a glimpse of Craven and gave him the most disdainful and disgusted look.

"Come for a little more thieving, have you, Craven?"

Paget was appalled by the way he spoke to them, but he dared not speak out.

"When I want to take something, I don't fail," sneered Craven.

"Perhaps not, but next time you do, I will be there to catch you. You are a stain on this army, Craven. A man without honour has no business wearing that uniform."

Paget could bear it no longer.

"How dare you, Sir!"

Rooke smiled as he let Paget go on, as if to hand him the rope with which to hang himself.

"You would dare call Major Craven's honour into

question, Sir? Shame on you!"

Rooke looked disappointed that Paget had not gone far enough to justify scolding him as severely as he would like, and so instead he turned his scorn on Craven.

"You see, Craven, when you do not maintain discipline, this is what you get, rabid dogs."

Paget was fuming and tried to move forward as if he wanted to pick a fight, but Craven held him back.

"It's okay, Lieutenant. The Major here is merely envious that we have actually fought the enemy, and not just gazed upon them from afar whilst better men risked their lives and bravely faced the enemy," declared Craven with a smirk.

Rooke did not like that. His back straightened, his head twitched to the side, and he coughed a little. Craven's experience of battle was hard to argue with, and yet Rooke was determined to find a way.

"A man may stand upon a battlefield and watch from afar. So very convenient that you are never at the front of the lines where a soldier should be. I have to wonder if you really ever took part at all, or if your men merely spread outrageous rumours of your dreamt up exploits to other drunks and fools like themselves."

Craven said nothing. He had nothing to prove as he watched Rooke desperately find some way to undermine him.

"Yes, a braggard and a dreamer."

"Were you there storming the breach?" Paget pointed to the repairs still underway on the fortress walls.

"Were you?" Rooke snarled back at him.

"Yes, I was, sword and pistol in hand and shoulder to shoulder with Major Craven. We were there when General

Craufurd was shot down, where were you?"

Rooke brushed off the question because he had nothing to brag about.

"Eager to get into the city first so you could get first pickings, were you? Get your hands on some Spanish women?" Rooke snarled as he walked away.

Paget tried to advance on him again and his hand reached for his sword, but once more Craven held him back. Matthys watched from afar and looked stunned and impressed at the restraint his old friend was showing. It was usually the Lieutenant who was the voice of reason and restraint.

"Sir, he insults us. He insults you," protested Paget.

"Yes, he does."

"And you will do nothing?"

"There is but one thing I could do, and I must not."

"Why, Sir? You are quite within your right to demand satisfaction for such insults."

"Yes, but what good would it do? Wellington needs every soldier he can muster, even the bad ones. We cannot fight amongst ourselves, not when we have so much work ahead of us."

"Spoken like a true tactician, like a true officer," added Matthys as he joined them.

"And if the insults continue?" Paget sounded worried.

"Rooke is harmless. An irritating fly, nothing more."

Paget groaned as he wasn't so sure. His honour and the reputation of them all meant so much that to have it tarnished boiled his blood, but he would not oppose Craven's decision. For that would only make him a hypocrite, and he despised that idea even more than the insults levelled at them.

"How long do you think until we march on?" Craven asked Matthys, who he still relied so heavily on for insight, just as he had done for so many years.

"It would make sense to wait a while and gather our strength and supplies, and this weather is still not kind."

"Then not for several more weeks?"

Matthys shook his head. "I wish I could say I knew the mind of Wellington, but I do not believe any man does, and perhaps we should feel lucky for that."

"Then we wait?"

"And suffer more insults," muttered Paget.

Craven groaned as he didn't much like it either, but as he looked back to the bellowing chimneys across the homes that had become the lodgings for the Army, he took a deep breath and reflected on how good they had it.

"We are alive. We have food and fire and roofs over our heads. Things could be much worse," he smiled.

Even Paget agreed. He had slummed it with the rest of them enough times over the years they had known one another that the privilege he once knew was a distant childhood memory.

"Then we will lay idle with nothing but one another's company to pass the time?"

Craven nodded in agreement before glancing cheekily at the horde of rum under heavy guard.

"That is not ours, and it never will be," insisted Matthys.

Craven groaned in agreement and said nothing more of it. The day passed quickly, as it was a relief to have no great chores or distance to travel. Craven fell into a deep sleep, warm and comfortable in their lodgings. The next thing he knew he was being shaken awake. He quickly reached for a weapon to find it was Paget. He relaxed and groaned as it was still dark outside.

"What is it?" he complained.

"It's Birback, Sir."

"What has he done this time?"

"Sir, you must come with me. I need your help," he said, hauling Craven from his bed before hurrying on.

Craven sighed exhaustively as he got up and pulled on his coat. He did not even bother with a weapon. There was no need of one as they were surrounded by an army of their own troops. He stepped out into the cold of the night to find it was bitter, and he winced, remembering how cosy and comfortable he had been.

"Where is he?"

"Follow me, Sir," insisted Paget as he ran on with much urgency. He was already out of hearing distance, and so Craven was forced to follow on without any answers.

Craven huffed angrily. He didn't want to take a step further and yet knew he must, because Paget would not have pulled him from his bed if it were not of great importance. Although he could hardly imagine what could be so vitally urgent, as there was not an enemy for miles around.

"This better be important," he grumbled.

He stumbled on and realised he was being led back to the mules carrying the vast supplies of rum. He began to shake his head, imagining what chaos he was about to find. Paget took cover behind a large barrel and pointed out towards the scene. The soldiers who had been appointed to protect the valuable goods were in fact the worst culprits of them all. Instead of guarding the rum, they had delved into it. They were already so drunk they could not even stand as they guzzled from the pigskins and fell about making fools of themselves. Craven smiled, knowing that could just as easily have been him, as it had in past times.

"Well, Sir?"

"Not my problem," shrugged Craven.

"But look, Sir."

Paget pointed to the drunken soldiers. Craven rubbed his weary eyes to get a better look when he realised what Paget was so concerned about. It was not that the soldiers had broken into the supplies they were ordered to protect, but that Birback was amongst them, drinking and laughing and making a fool of himself. He began to sing loudly and merrily before springing up from the crate he was sitting on to blast the tune from his lungs, only to stumble and fall for how drunk he was.

"Damned fool. He'll get the lash for that if he is caught, or worse," gasped Craven.

"What do we do, Sir?"

"Get him the hell out of there."

"Are we not complicit then, too?"

"We already are. As officers in this army, we both have a duty to put an end to this and see that they are punished."

"Yes, we do, then we are to report it and let them all suffer for their crimes?"

"Not a chance," scowled Craven, "Come on."

He rushed on towards their drunken friend. Paget hesitated for a moment as he looked around like a naughty schoolboy expecting to be caught by his headmaster at any moment. But he looked back to see Craven pressing on without any fear and felt compelled to follow. He quickly caught up with the Major who was still half awake.

"What if we are caught, Sir? Will we not face even more severe punishment as those who should have taken charge of this situation?" Paget whispered.

"There is a good rule to remember when enacting a crime, Lieutenant. Don't get caught," smiled Craven.

Even the utterance of the word crime and its association with him made Paget uncomfortable. He once again looked all around in fear of being caught. Both men wore their greatcoats and nothing upon their heads, which at least made them difficult to identify from a distance. But hiding in the shadows was not something Paget was either accustomed to or comfortable with. He liked to stand tall and proud and have all know who he was and be worthy of a good reputation. They reached the drunken soldiers to find they were in a dreadful state. Few were able to stand, and they continued to drink, spilling it down their gluttonous faces without a care in the world.

"Come on, let's get you out of here." Craven tried to put a hand on Birback to help him up, only to have it pushed violently and angrily away.

"Get off me!"

His words were slurred, and he swung so wildly it took him off balance. He fell from the crate he was perched upon, landing headfirst on the cold and wet ground. Craven tried to help him up, but Birback lashed out with a back handed blow which struck Craven's jaw, snapping his head aside. Birback began to laugh as he propped himself onto the crate once more and reached for one of the pigskins to get another fill.

"You are coming with us, now," growled Craven.

"To hell I am," he replied as he pulled the cap from the wineskin to drink more, but instead it was Craven's fist which connected with his lips. Birback fell back unconscious, dropping the wineskin and causing the rum to spill out across the ground.

"Why did you do that, Sir?"

"Because I have been where he is, and I know how difficult he was going to be."

Craven picked up the wineskin still spilling its contents. He took a sniff of the rum. It wasn't the best, but it was better than nothing.

"What are you doing, Sir?"

Craven took a mouthful before placing the cap back on and throwing it aside.

"It would be a shame to waste it, don't you think?"

"Sir, that belongs to the Army."

"It was spilling out over the ground, and so it belonged to no one but the earth."

He tried to lift Birback up. He was a big, heavy man and a dead weight considering he was unconscious.

"Here, help me," he ordered Paget who still looked deeply uncomfortable with the entire situation, but he did as ordered, even though he was repulsed by the awful smell of the drunken Scotsman. They each took an arm and braced him across their shoulders, dragging him away, his feet trailing across the ground behind them.

"The men who did this will have a lot to answer for in the morning," muttered Paget.

"Yes, and so not another word of this, you hear me? We were never here, and neither was he," replied Craven, referring to Birback.

"How can we hide it? An unconscious ox reeking of rum. There will be no keeping this secret, Sir."

"Amongst the Salfords there will. We protect our own, do we not?"

"We do, but I am not sure he deserves it."

"No, he doesn't, but I won't see him flogged for being a fool. Those men guarding the mules had a duty to protect that rum, and instead they chose to dip into it. Birback only joined a celebration that was already underway."

"I am not exactly sure that is how it happened, Sir."

"Did you see how it happened?"

"Well, no…"

"Then that is how it happened. He will sleep it off and live with the regret of a throbbing head all day tomorrow. That will be punishment enough."

"Is it, Sir?"

"You would see him put to the lash?"

"Well, no, Sir. I mean it is probably the correct thing to do, but…" he hesitated.

"I have made more than enough mistakes, more than most I'd say, but we need not pay a stiff price for the foolish and harmless ones."

They could still hear the roar of laughter from the drunken rabble they had left behind, but soon enough they were out of earshot and far enough away that they would not be associated with those soldiers' crimes. Paget breathed a sigh of relief.

"Give me a minute," he pleaded. He was struggling under the weight of the burly Scotsman.

They placed him down and Craven smiled before beginning to laugh at the absurdity of the situation.

"I am afraid I don't see the funny side, Sir."

"You knew what Birback was doing was wrong, and yet

you came to me to help him shirk his punishments, why is that?"

"I...I'm not sure, Sir."

"Because you care about the soldiers who fight beside you, and I cannot think of a more valuable asset for any soldier to have, let alone an officer."

"You think shirking my duties as an officer is a good quality?"

"I think doing what is right is not always doing what the law or the Army says it is."

"But how can you be the judge of that?"

"Same as everything else in life, we do our best with the knowledge we have. Remember when you first came to us, you hated the way I operated, and yet in time you came to respect it. It was not your way nor the way you had been told was correct or proper, but you could see that it worked. Don't think for a minute that the generals of this army do not bend and break the rules as it suits them. Sometimes for the best, and sometimes not."

Paget sighed with exhaustion.

"I used to think it was so easy. I learnt to live by the rules, Sir. When you know what to do and what not to do, and the clear line between the two, then life is all so very easy."

"And now you can see that life is not that way?"

Paget nodded in agreement.

"A lesson you learn at a very young age when you are not born with all the wealth one could dream of."

"I suppose so, Sir, but it is hard for me to imagine such a thing."

"No, it isn't. You might have lived a rich life as a boy, but as a man out here, you have lived what the rest of us do.

Surviving in the worst of conditions with nothing more than what you can carry. You could have transferred out of here a long time ago, and to a far more comfortable position with better chances of promotion. Back to the life of a Lord, but you stayed, wading through the mud and blood with the rest of us. That speaks volumes to me, my friend. Most soldiers trudge on because they have no choice not to, but you chose to stay."

"I came here to fight, and with you, Sir, I am best placed to do so."

"Well, you certainly came to the right place. I have been fighting my whole life, and only death will stop me."

"Don't jest about such a thing, Sir."

Craven smiled, for the Lieutenant was such a gentle soul.

"Come on, let's get out of this damn cold."

They hauled Birback up. He suddenly came around and peered about in a confused state.

"Where is the rum?" he grumbled in barely legible slurs.

"You drank it all," replied Craven.

Birback groaned in agreement as that made sense. He smiled like a madman.

"Yes, I did," he declared, grinning at them both.

"Listen to me. I will repeat this tomorrow when there is a greater chance of you remembering, but I will say it now. You were never there, and you did not drink the rum. Do you understand me?"

Birback didn't seem to care, and so Craven slapped him across the face, causing him to wake up a little more sharply.

"What was that for?"

"Mr Paget took a great risk to save you from the wrath which all who broke into those rum rations will suffer tomorrow. He owes you nothing, and yet he did this for you. I will not have him suffer because of it. Do you understand me?"

"Yes," he replied sheepishly.

"You are going straight to bed, and you will not step foot outside again until you are sober and do not stink, do you understand?"

"That might be some time," replied Paget.

"Yes, it will," smirked Birback before belching loudly, causing Paget to wince from disgust at the revolting smell.

"You're a beast," declared Craven.

"I am," admitted Birback proudly.

They helped him back to their lodging where they found Matthys awake and waiting for them. Yet he said nothing as they dragged Birback to his bed. They threw him down like a sack, and he was out cold once more within seconds. Craven climbed back into bed, but Paget took a seat beside Matthys.

"All is well?" Matthys asked.

"As good as it can be," admitted Paget.

"You did a good thing tonight."

Paget breathed a sigh of relief. It meant a lot coming from a man with such a robust moral compass.

"I was not so sure. Choosing between my responsibilities as an officer and my duty to my fellow soldier, or friend even, if you could call him that."

"We cannot let our friends off from all crimes, but a little leeway and understanding is quite appropriate, especially after what we've seen and done in days past," replied Matthys as he thought back to the assault on the breach.

"Thank you."

It was just what he needed to hear. He hated battling with

his inner conflicts and would much prefer a real fight with an enemy where nothing was in doubt.

CHAPTER 3

Craven got up from his bed and looked out of a window. Hawkshaw was staring out in a melancholic state towards the fortress walls and the breach where they had buried General Craufurd. He looked back to see Matthys had some demands in his eyes. Craven knew what the Sergeant wanted of him.

"We all went through it," grumbled Craven.

"Yes, and it affects every man differently. You are as tough as an ox, but remember, even you had your breaking point. It's hard to remember how dark those days were now."

"I remember," groaned Craven, remembering them like they were yesterday.

"It took a lot to break you out of that jail you had made for yourself. Everything we had and more."

"And you think my brother is in the same place?"

"I think he is marching firmly on that path, yes."

"But when I was in such a way, we knew why, but for him,

it seems to be everything about this war which troubles him. How can we fix that when we will soon march on and have so many battles ahead of us?"

Matthys sighed in frustration. "I wish I knew, for all our sakes."

"A good walk could do no harm," smiled Craven.

He went forward to his brother and was joined by Paget, who upon seeing something was happening was eager to be a part of it, no matter what it was. Hawkshaw jumped a little as he realised he was not alone, having been lost in his thoughts.

"I think a stretch of the legs is in order, and perhaps we should take a good stroll through the fortress and admire what we have achieved?" Craven asked.

Hawkshaw agreed. He was not particularly eager at the idea, but glad to take his mind away from wherever it had wandered. Matthys nodded in appreciation at seeing how compassionate Craven had become in recent times as he watched the three officers start their walk.

"It was a great victory to finally take this city. It reminds me of Talavera, after which we were riding so high it felt like we were unstoppable," declared Craven.

"Yes, and now that seems such a distant memory," admitted Paget.

"But we have a second chance to relive what that campaign should have been. We should have marched all the way to Madrid and celebrated in the streets as liberators. That can still come, and this was the first step to that great day."

"It's a long way to Madrid, for we are barely a few steps into Spain," replied Hawkshaw.

"And I fear we have been here before, only to be driven

back," added Paget.

"But not defeated, and that is what matters. We choose our battles carefully and we keep winning, and that is how we will go on. Even if we have to take a step back, we will always go forward once more," insisted Craven.

"I don't know how you can remain in such high spirits. For there is no end to this war in sight, only more death," sobbed Hawkshaw.

"You are a soldier, and this is a war, how it could be otherwise?"

"Perhaps I am a fool who expected things to be different. I came here for an honourable fight. Mostly I came here to fight you, but now we are locked in this eternal cycle of bloodshed."

Craven looked to Paget, pleading with him to try and help. He could find no more soothing words, as ultimately, he was right. Paget's heart was breaking for the Captain, who he had much come to respect and rely on, and so he dug deep into his soul and tried to find a way to reach out to the man.

"There are still honourable days and times ahead of us all. War might not be all that you expected it to be, but any man who says otherwise is a fool or a liar. This all came as a great surprise to all of us but let us not forget that has never really changed. The great victories of the past were won in the same fashion, paid for in blood. But it is still honourable. For we do not fight to cause bloodshed, but to put an end to it. We fight for the people of Portugal and Spain, and of England, too. For Napoleon would take the whole world if soldiers like us did not stand up and say no, we will not tolerate this behaviour. You would stand up and protect a person who was offended or ridiculed or struck at the dinner table or in the street, would you not?"

"Yes, of course."

"Fighting the armies of Napoleon is no different. He would bully and enslave us all, and I will not stand for that, and I don't think you would either."

Craven looked to Paget in deep appreciation, astonished at the eloquence of the young Lieutenant, whose tongue was as skilful as his hand was with a sword, something Craven could only dream of.

"But the horrors, they are there for us to see, and commit and live through."

"Yes, they are, and that is our cross to bear, but it is not the end, merely the road. We will get through it, and we will return to England as heroes and to peace."

Hawkshaw nodded in agreement, warming a little to the idea and relaxed slightly as they walked on.

"You have a wondrous way with words, Mr Paget. One might think you have the intention to enter politics," smiled Craven.

"My father would have wanted precisely that, an honourable service in the Army, followed by a time in Parliament, or at least he used to. Now I imagine he would block such a plan with all the powers at his disposal, which are a great many."

"And you, is that what you want?"

"I thought I did," pondered Paget.

"But not anymore?" Hawkshaw asked curiously, sensing the same doubts in Paget's voice as he struggled with.

"This war will change us all, for better and for worse, and when I do go home to England for good, it will not be to take on such new responsibilities."

"Then what will you do?"

"With my father's money I could have done anything. I could have not worked another day and lived a life of leisure, but now? I must support myself, and I suppose a lifelong career in the Army might well lay ahead of me."

"You would live like this for the rest of your life?"

"It will not always be like this. We live in the most difficult of days, but for most soldiers, they live out their days in peace in England or some other postings to some far away and exciting land without war," mused Paget.

"It's true. Many soldiers go their entire lives without seeing war," agreed Craven.

"Then I suppose we have the very worst of luck," smiled Hawkshaw.

"Have you ever thought it is not bad luck, but that we are the very best men for these times? That we were chosen?" Paget asked.

Craven chuckled as it seemed absurd.

"If lesser men had filled our shoes, perhaps Napoleon would already be in England?"

"You think we are better than our forebears?" Hawkshaw asked.

"Not all of them, no, but perhaps some men are destined to sit in the barracks all their lives, and not suited to anything more, but others are for more and rise when they are needed?"

"You are talking about the soul of a warrior? Passed down through generations, as though we were the Celts fighting the Romans?"

"Yes, Sir," smiled Paget.

"I'll remind you that the Romans won, and Napoleon sees himself as the next Roman Emperor, for he already carries the title and marches eagles across Europe."

"He is no Roman Emperor," seethed Paget.

Hawkshaw laughed at the Lieutenant's abrupt anger, and it was a joy to hear. It was the first time any of them had heard it from him in as long as they could remember. They walked on in good spirits as they made their way into the city. It was a bustling place as many of the locals had returned. Engineers continued to rebuild and improve the defences with large work parties drawn up from the unfortunate infantry, a task Craven and his Salford Rifles were saved from. They could not be called upon for such duties, or at least they had gotten away with such chores so far.

"It took a great deal to secure this city. I pray we do not have to relinquish it ever again," admitted Paget.

"If we do, it is because we have abandoned this war and left for England," replied Craven.

"How can you be so sure, Sir?"

"Because Wellington knows it and he has spoken of it. England will not keep financing this war if they do not see progress."

"And yet they will not provide enough money and men to get that progress," Hawkshaw said, "You both know as well as I how many regiments sit idle at home."

"For the defence of the realm," protested Paget.

"Is that not what the fencibles are for? The yeomanry and the militia and all of the volunteers? A great army with the single purpose of defending the borders, why then do regular regiments sit at home and do nothing? Take the 2nd North

British Dragoons."

"The Scots Greys?" piped up Paget excitedly as he imagined the great big dragoons on their huge chargers, the closest thing in the British Army to the knights of old.

"Yes, they have not served abroad since the Low Countries, almost twenty years. Year after year this war goes on, and Wellington is not sent the might he needs to truly crush the enemy."

"I wish I knew the minds of those who make such decisions, but I do not," admitted Craven.

"Look who it is, Sir." Paget pointed forward to Captain Ferreira. He was sitting in the warming sunlight atop a barrel at the side of the street, watching the world go by in blissful calm.

"What trouble have you come looking for?" he asked with a grumble as if their presence had already disturbed the peace.

"No trouble here."

"And I suppose there was none last night, either?"

"I don't know of what you speak," replied Craven innocently.

"The men appointed to guard a great horde of mules carrying rum decided to help themselves to their fill, and they surely did get their fill. For some of those men drank themselves to an early death and would wake no more this morning."

"Truly?" Paget asked in horror.

Hawkshaw sighed in frustration. "Soldiers who survived the siege and assault of this fortress only to die over nothing?"

"They are not the first. I hear some men fell into great vats of rum here in the city after the assault and drowned there," replied Ferreira.

"Doesn't sound like such a terrible way to go," Craven

chuckled.

"How can you say that, Sir?" Paget gasped.

"Many great soldiers have died merely of dysentery, shitting themselves to death. I'd take drowning in rum, wouldn't you?"

Paget was disgusted by the concept, but Ferreira saw the funny side and laughed aloud.

"There was another amongst the guards of those mules, another soldier who indulged himself but was nowhere to be found by the provosts this morning," added Ferreira.

"Oh, really?" Paget asked in a hilariously suspicious way, as he was too honest a man to be an effective liar.

"We all know who that soldier was, and he would be wise to be more careful."

"Not much chance of that," sighed Craven.

"I don't know why men do it," moaned Paget.

"They can't help themselves. See, there is probably one right there, trading for a little rum." Ferreira gestured towards a side street where a British cavalryman exchanged something with another man not in uniform for a pigskin. He looked suspiciously around and noticed the four officers gathered around, his face turning pale.

"You, stop right there!" Paget angrily charged towards the cavalryman.

"Here we go," smirked Ferreira.

"Leave him be, will you?" Craven pleaded.

The man panicked and tried to flee, and Paget was right on after him, causing Craven to sigh and follow him as he would not let any harm come to the Lieutenant. The cavalryman did not get far as he found himself at a dead end and turned back to face them. His hand reached for his sword.

"I wouldn't," declared Craven as Paget stopped short and took hold of his sword with both hands; the left about the scabbard and the right on the grip so that he could retrieve the blade in a flash if need be.

The cavalryman, seeing he was outnumbered and in the presence of so many officers, backed down, though it made Craven chuckle. He knew Paget could have handled the man singlehandedly.

"Give that here!" Paget demanded.

"It's mine. I did not steal it, but purchased it in a fair trade," protested the man.

"Now!"

The cavalryman sighed and handed it over, and upon opening the pigskin a waft of rum passed over Paget's nose.

"I haven't done anything wrong, Sir, just trading for a little rum to keep my bones warm on a cold night, not whilst I am on duty or anything like that," declared the man, trying to defend himself and get back what was his. But Paget was having none of it as he looked back to the man whom he had traded with.

"And what did you trade him for it?"

The cavalryman groaned, knowing he had been caught as Paget made his way to find out. The suspicious cavalryman pursued him, hoping to keep the contents of the bag a secret.

"It is nothing, Sir, just a little food," he claimed.

But Paget ripped the bag from the man's hands and opened it to see it was a bag of cracked corn. He knew precisely what he was looking at, for this was no innocent bag of goods.

"This is feed for a horse!"

"A little extra I had to spare, Sir."

Paget did not believe him. He thrust the pigskin back into the other man's arms and got hold of the bag of corn.

"Leave him be, Paget," said Craven.

But he would not let it go.

"Take me to your horse, now!"

"Sir, but I…" began the man.

"Now!"

Craven breathed a deep sigh, knowing this situation was not going to get any better. They followed Paget and the cavalryman on, even Ferreira trailed after them with much curiosity.

"Are you sure you want to cause this much trouble?" Craven asked the Lieutenant.

"I am sure I could not turn a blind eye, yes," snapped Paget.

They were led outside into the fields beyond where the cavalry's horses were mostly kept, anchored to the ground by ropes and iron pins. Many cavalrymen who were seeing to their horses gazed over at the odd party of officers leading one of their own, as if by the point of the sword, though none had their blade drawn. Soon enough they came to the suspicious man's horse, but he would not look at it as his eyes gazed at the floor in shame. The animal was miserably thin. It was not the only animal in such a state, but it was the one Paget had an understanding as to why. He gazed over at some of the other cavalrymen in sight, few of which would meet his gaze. He felt physically repulsed as he looked down at the bag of feed which rightfully belonged to the starving animal, and then his fury turned back to the cavalryman responsible.

"You would trade this fine animal's meal for rum?" he

accused the man.

"I am sorry, Sir, but it is the first time I have made such an offence. I had a lapse of judgement."

Paget was having none of it. This was not a horse who had missed a day of feed but many.

"The way this animal looks tells a different tale from what comes from your tongue, for he has long had the bitters and you the sweet," seethed Paget.

"It is just a horse, Sir."

"Just a horse!"

Paget stormed forward in a rare outburst and struck the man with a heavy blow with the back of his hand, causing the cavalryman to stagger and barely stay on his feet. Hawkshaw could barely believe what he was seeing. He had never seen Paget strike a man who did not threaten him first, but the Lieutenant was seething with anger to such an extent he was shaking with rage. Through his love of his horse, Augustus, he could imagine such a man stealing feed from his best friend and how that made him want to murder the man standing before him. In that moment he hated the cavalryman more than he had ever hated any Frenchman. There was an awkward silence as Paget panted angrily, and nobody dared get in his way as he pondered his next step.

"I would challenge you to single combat if you were an officer, and if you were an enemy, I would strike you down where you stand, but you are neither of those things."

He seethed before looking out at some of the man's comrades who watched on. Paget looked back at the malnourished horse and several others that were in little better condition, leading him to suspect many others were trading their animals' supplies for their own treats. His eyes were red with rage. He could barely contain himself as he tried desperately to maintain the dignity and measure of an officer and decide what was the correct course of action, for he would not let it go unpunished.

"He's had enough. You have made your point," declared Hawkshaw.

But Paget shook his head.

"Oh, no, not nearly enough. If a man will not do the right thing of his own accord, then he must be forced to do so. You have made me do what I prayed I would never have to do. You made me do this, by your despicable conduct. I will use the one power left at my disposal. You are to be lashed."

Craven's expression turned to despair as the situation was rapidly descending into chaos.

"You cannot do this," declared Hawkshaw.

"I can and I will."

Craven stepped up beside him and whispered as he tried to calm the situation.

"This is not within your power. His commanding officer must decide his fate."

"Bring me a whip!"

Nobody moved. Yet he spotted a riding whip on a saddle nearby and drew it out.

"Strip!" he cried out to the cavalryman.

The man looked to Craven as the most senior officer to make some appeal, but he found no sympathy there.

"You are going to let him do this?" Hawkshaw asked Craven.

Craven shrugged as he did not want to intervene, and

frankly, he agreed to the punishment. The cavalryman took off his tunic and shirt, stripping to the waist. Lashes were normally delivered in a ceremony with the soldier's unit formed up and the man tied to a tripod created by lashing three spontoons together. This was a rather more informal affair, which Paget had no right or authority to conduct, but that did not stop him.

"Kneel!"

The man did as ordered and exposed his bare back.

"Fifty lashes, that is a mere fraction of what you deserve for this heinous crime, and let it be a lesson to you all!"

For a moment he paused as his fellow officers watched on, thinking he might hesitate and give up the show, but he raised the whip and smashed it down onto the man's skin. A flogging was always a horrible sight, and yet one which had been used to maintain discipline widely throughout the Army. Paget had never thought he would see the day that he would enforce it. He believed in a better way, by rewarding men, not punishing them, but he had been driven over the edge and now went on delivering the punishment. He had delivered a dozen lashes and opened the man's flesh when tears began to stream down his face. For he was now as disgusted by the sight and of his own actions as he was of the man's treatment of the horse. He dealt one more lash against the man's back before dropping the whip as he could not stomach to do anymore.

"Enough!" he roared as much to himself as he did to bring an end to the man's suffering and anguish.

"You did a truly monstrous thing, and I will not suffer to see such done to any animal. Never let this happen again. Not because of your fear of being caught, but for the disgust you should feel for stooping so low."

Paget stormed away as several of the cavalryman's comrades came to his aid to help with his wounds. Paget made several hundred yards at a brisk pace before breaking down in tears and crumpling to the ground. Craven and the others soon caught up but did not know how to deal with the situation.

"What have I done?"

"What your conscience required."

"You think I was right to do it, Sir?" Paget begged.

"I think the Army needs more men with as much compassion as you have, and you need not apologise for being the way you are."

Hawkshaw and Ferreira exchanged concerned glances, knowing there could be severe repercussions for what the Lieutenant had done. He had stepped far beyond the powers of his position.

"What punishment will I suffer for this?"

"Probably nothing at all. That man would be wise to never mention any of this. For he will have to admit to his own crimes in order to attempt to sully your name."

"That is what I have become? That is what it comes to? I can get away with a crime because the victim cannot come forward?"

Craven knelt down and hauled him to his feet so that he would stand tall and proud as he always did.

"Did that man deserve what you did?"

"Yes, that and worse, but I would not see it done."

"Then you did the right thing. Had you gone to that man's commanding officer, he would have seen to the fifty lashes, and they would have been done to completion with the cat o' nine tails. You did what must be done and saved that man far worse a punishment."

Paget was a little relieved to hear it.

"Truly?" He looked to Ferreira and Hawkshaw for confirmation.

Hawkshaw merely shrugged, still stunned by the outburst of violence by the kindest man he knew, but Ferreira was in firm agreement.

"A terrible thing, but war is full of terrible things. You did no wrong, and need not feel any shame," insisted Craven.

Paget breathed a sigh of relief as he gathered himself.

"What this war makes of us all," he muttered.

"Indeed," admitted Hawkshaw, who now looked out into the open air with the same blank and lost expression as he had done earlier that morning.

CRAVEN'S WAR – THE FINAL CHANCE

CHAPTER 4

"Lieutenant Paget!" a voice cried out.

The cry awoke Craven and several others, including Paget. Craven leapt to his feet with his sword in hand as he peered out of the window to see three cavalry officers standing outside.

"What is it?"

"I don't know, but I can hazard a pretty good guess."

Paget stepped up beside him to look for himself, but Craven placed himself protectively between the Lieutenant and the door.

"What can they want, Sir?"

"You struck one of their own, and I imagine they aren't too happy about it."

"You said the man would stay silent?"

"If he were smart, but I don't think there was much smart about that man, and a great many witnesses, too."

Paget groaned uncomfortably.

"Those officers must not have been ignorant of the crimes their men were committing, and that makes them complicit. Do not apologise. You owe them nothing."

"Lieutenant Paget!" roared one of the officers once more, "Will you not come and face us?"

"I will not hide."

"No, and you should not, but you owe those men nothing, and they can take from you nothing." Craven still blocked the way to the door as Paget got fully dressed and came up to pass him, but Craven would not move.

"I do not need you to protect me, Sir. This is my quarrel, and I will deal with it as an officer and a gentleman."

Craven groaned in agreement before stepping aside. Paget hauled the door open and stepped outside into the brisk morning air. All three officers wore the blue tunics of the light cavalry and did not even wear their greatcoats, as if to make a show of who they were with their bright dolman jackets. All were young junior officers, and the man at the centre was the leader of the pack. He was of a similar age and build as Paget, but with bright blond hair. He bore no scars of war and his uniform so clean, he'd either had it recently replaced or had not been on campaign for long, of which the latter seemed the most likely. All three proudly wore the broad bladed and heavily curved sabre with characterise P shaped minimalist guard, which General Le Marchant had pioneered and so heavily campaigned to become the standard across all of the cavalry. He had got half of what he wanted, as it was only the soldiers of the light cavalry and horse artillery who used them, but they displayed them with pride as an elite symbol.

"I am he," declared Paget as Craven stepped up to support

him.

"You had one of ours flogged. I hear you even did it yourself."

"What of it?"

Paget no longer felt any shame or regret for his actions.

"My name is Lieutenant Cleeves. When I learnt that one of my troopers, William Sympher, had suffered lashes and was recovering his wounds, I wondered why, and how I could not have known about such an incident. Well, I got to the bottom of it. You dared strike one of our own? The incredulousness of it!"

Paget said nothing as the man went on.

"I explained the matter to my Colonel, and he said the matter was over and there was nothing to be done for it, but that would not do. And so I took this matter further until I reached Wellington himself, and do you know what I was told? I was told to drop the matter, and why would that be? Because you are a family friend to our General and protected by him. Special treatment the likes of which many colonels would be lucky to receive. And so, I have no recourse left, I will find no justice from the Army."

"Your man was stealing the feed of his horse in exchange for rum, and it was not the first time. Some of the men in your troop let their horses starve so they may enjoy sweets, and you could not have been ignorant of this."

"I know what Sympher did, but it was not your place to take action!"

"It was me or nobody else. To know what that man was doing and do nothing was to shirk your responsibility as an officer, as a cavalryman, and as a gentleman."

Cleeves smiled as though he had gotten what he was looking for.

"Shit," whispered Craven.

"You insult my integrity and all of my virtues as a gentleman and as a soldier, and for that I demand satisfaction," stated Cleeves as he called Paget out in a duel.

"I accept, but I warn you, it is the greatest mistake of your life," replied Paget confidently.

"We meet at noon behind the first barn on the road West, you know it?"

"I do."

"And your choice of weapon? Englishmen duel with pistols, but I say it is weak."

Craven smiled as Cleeves was indeed making the greatest mistake of his life, just as Paget had said. Only a fool would challenge such a fine swordsman to a clash with blades.

"Let us use the old ways, then, and settle this matter with cold steel."

"I suppose you will use that regimental spit?" seethed Cleeves, referring to the infantry spadroon which Paget used, a sword ridiculed by many a cavalryman for being so light, but he knew as well as any other that it was also so nimble it could run circles around a cavalry sword in battle on foot.

"Let no man say you lost unfairly. Lend me one of your sabres, and we will fight as equals, at least in the tools which we wield."

"I'll be expecting you. Don't be late, or worse still, run from your responsibilities."

"I will be there," insisted Paget.

Cleeves smirked as if he had won a great victory before

turning and walking away with a great swagger. His comrades celebrated as if he had already overcome his adversary. Paget was just shaking his head in disbelief.

"Is that what you wanted?"

"No, Sir, but it is out of my hands. For I only spoke the truth and that man took offence."

"You can't kill him. You do know that?"

"I don't mean to. He is a fool, not an enemy," sniffled Paget.

There was a sadness in his voice, and he seemed distant.

"Do you regret it? Getting involved with the matter of the horse's feed?"

"No, not at all. I only lament the fact it was necessary for me to do so. That sad state of affairs should never have been allowed to happen. Now we fight because one proud fool will not do what is right and instead risks his life to save face. How foolish some men are."

"That is the story of our entire history, I am afraid. Pride is often more important than all else, and none of us are entirely free of its hold, not even you."

"You think I am wrong to fight that man?"

"Oh, no, not at all, though I suspect Matthys would say I am the very last person to judge that. I do not have the best history when it comes to duelling, at least in the eyes of many a man with high morals such as him," smiled Craven.

"Like this war, I was not the cause of it, and I would see it ended tomorrow if I had such a power, but whilst it has to be fought, I will fight it."

"What is all of this noise about?" Matthys stepped out into the morning light and yawned.

"Nothing of importance," replied Craven.

"You are a damn bad liar."

"I've been called far worse."

"If you must do this, then just be sure of two things, and you will be right with the Lord, both in heaven and Wellington."

"What is that?" Paget asked curiously.

"Do not kill that man and do not die yourself."

Craven laughed, though he knew it was true.

"How can I be sure not to kill a man when we fight with sabres that would cleave a man in twain?"

"A man can survive many a cut, though you should not strike him so hard that you might remove an arm or his head," replied Matthys.

"And do not give point. For a man may far more likely expire from a thrust than a cut," added Craven.

"That is half of my repertoire," protested Paget.

"You have plenty more knowledge than that," declared Craven.

"Does the point really kill more often, Sir?"

"Yes, for most wounds of the edge are merely sewn up and most men recover, but the point may cause uncurable damage inside a man's body and make impossible work for the surgeon, and risk far worse infection also."

"And yet our cavalrymen have a great affection for the cut?"

"Yes, because killing a man is not always the most important goal. Striking first, incapacitating the enemy, striking without being struck oneself. What good is the most fatal wound delivered when it cannot stop the riposte?"

"Then the cut is better than the thrust?"

Craven laughed as it was an age-old argument which they had all had so many times.

"Not at all, but I fear this is an argument that will rage on for well beyond our lifetimes, even if we were to live one hundred years!"

Paget looked to Matthys as if to seek his forgiveness for accepting the duel.

"I hope you do not think ill of me for this," he muttered.

"Not every battle is wrong nor evil. You did not bring this upon yourself by doing the wrong thing. Far from it. You did a good deed, and this evil that has followed will not overcome you, not whilst you remain true and do as I said."

"What else should I do in preparation?"

"Do not go into the fight cold, not in the body or mind. We have been idle for days. Take up the singlesticks and get your body moving. Practice within the limitations which you know you must conduct yourself."

The gravity of the situation was finally dawning on Paget. He had gotten himself into a life-or-death situation, and one with even worse consequences if he was to be the cause of the man's death, despite knowing his own life was in danger.

"Will you do that with me, Sir?"

"Of course," replied Craven as he went to find the training sticks, and Paget became lost in his own thoughts.

"I wish men could be better. That they could be more compassionate and more reasonable," he declared.

"Mr Paget, these are my worries every day for as long as I can remember," smiled Matthys.

"Well, how can we make it so? How can we change things for the better?"

"We can lead by example and encourage others to do the same."

"And those who will not change?"

"We have the power to change with both our voice and our blades."

Paget was surprised to hear it.

"I am always curious how such a righteous believer as you could be comfortable with killing."

"When it is right and just there is no evil in it. That is what we must always ask ourselves before attempting to take a life, and if you could not justify it before the Lord, then you know in your heart that it is wrong. Just like this cavalryman you go to test yourself against, you must not kill him. For the Lord would never forgive you, and neither would I."

Paget was lost in thought for a moment as he had so much to think about. The prospect of entering into a fight for life and limb used to be a simple if daunting one, but now he had to concern himself with how a different type of sword might affect his technique. How he may defend himself without dealing a fatal blow, and the severe consequences if he did not do everything exactly as he must.

"Here." Craven thrust a singlestick into his body.

Paget took the stick as they got a bit more space from their lodgings. Many of their comrades amassed to watch the display, having little else to occupy their minds and time. Craven snapped a quick cut to Paget's arm, and the blow smarted, for he did not even have time to react.

"You are distracted."

"I have much to be distracted by."

"It need not be so complicated. Defend yourself and

deliver blows which will not kill your man. That is all."

"Is it so easy?"

"Yes, and no," smiled Craven.

"Please, just tell me what I must know. For I have too many things occupying my mind and feel that my head may yet explode if they are not reduced to some palatable quantity."

Craven nodded in acceptance.

"The sabres you will use are very different to what you are accustomed. The total weight is not so much greater, but where that weight is placed is a world apart. The sabres of our light cavalrymen carry so much of their weight forward, towards the tip. This means they strike with tremendous power, but they are not so easily stopped or turned in a new direction. You will need to use great big circle parades to bring the blade around as you recover from cuts, and even to make cuts after your feints, like this."

Craven reached forward with a long reaching cut before whirling the tip of the blade in a great big circle so that it returned to its starting position.

"This is how you remain fast with a front heavy blade. Let the weight roll through into the next action. Do not fight it by attempting to stop one movement and begin another as you may so easily do with that spadroon of yours."

Paget replicated the move. It seemed alien to him. He was so accustomed to agile blades he could toss and turn with precise and quick motions and no concern for the weapon providing any resistance against him.

"You may not land a thrust, but your man does not know that. So whilst you may not strike with the point, you may threaten and feint with it, provoking your enemy in just the same way as if you had a foil in hand. Only the attack which follows must be with the edge."

"I can do that."

Paget had used similar actions many times before. He just had to remember not to use so much of the repertoire he had learnt with the express purpose of delivering fatal blows. The two came into their guard positions, and Paget took a deep breath. He concentrated fully as to not be struck again before they began to launch attack and riposte. Initially, they started slow, using barely half of their power and speed in what looked more like a staged fight before a theatre audience, but as they warmed up, the speed and intensity increased until it began to look like a serious affair. Charlie watched intently from the sidelines.

"Don't worry about him. He will handle himself just fine," said Ferreira compassionately.

She huffed with irritation.

"Of course, he will, but we should not be wasting our time fighting amongst ourselves when the French are out there. That is where we should direct our skill and our swords."

Ferreira was surprised. He had assumed she was concerned for his wellbeing. For knowledge of the relationship between the two was a poorly kept secret now amongst the closest friends in the regiment.

"We will soon enough, when the time is right."

"The time is always right," she growled.

Ferreira smiled. She was as feisty as ever, perpetually eager to get her hands on the enemy and spill their blood, but he fully understood her reasoning and could not disagree.

Craven continued to press the same information upon

Paget, insisting he treat the singlestick as though it were tip heavy, and use it in such a different manner as he was disposed and trained for. Soon enough the fight became a flowing dance of great rotations. The change in mechanics did not make for a slow fight by any means, but one of whirling blades swinging from one rotation into another in a most energetic fashion. As opposed to the refined and short motions that were so typical of the lighter straight swords both men typically carried. With every minute that passed, he was getting more comfortable and began to look natural with his movements. Finally, Craven brought a stop to it all.

"Enough, you must be warm, supple, and confident in your actions, but we must not press you to exhaustion."

It was not long before they had to be on their way, but the party with Paget remained small. They could not risk amassing great crowds and drawing the eyes of Wellington and his staff, or anyone else who might try and intervene. Craven was of course by his side, and so was Matthys, Charlie, Ferreira, and Vicenta, who was always eager to see such an exhibition.

"Will you act as my seconds?" he asked Craven and Ferreira, as only the officers could do so.

"Of course," replied Craven.

"Yes, though I cannot imagine there will be much work for us to do, except for perhaps intervening if that idiot's comrades attempt to join the affray."

"That would be a grave mistake," agreed Craven.

"For us all, for this must remain a matter between gentlemen, and this afternoon we must move on with no further words spoken on the matter," added Matthys.

"Indeed. The last thing we need is more trouble following

us. We have only just left all that behind," admitted Craven.

They rode on. The ground was soft under the hooves of their horses, and they could hear the mud squelch with every step, something any keen swordsman would keep a keen eye on. The knowledge of the ground could make all the difference between success and failure, life and death. It was a bleak thick cloud cover and little daylight to warm the troops who were not huddled about fires.

A dark day for dark deeds. I have no desire to hurt my opponent. I only wanted the man to stand up and do the right thing.

Paget was more disappointed than angry, for he thought so much more highly of the officers of the British Army than some of them were acting of late.

The road was relatively quiet as the supply wagons struggled in the soft mud. Often moving at a snail's pace as they brought provisions to the front line that Ciudad Rodrigo had become. Soon enough the barn came into view, and as they led their horses off the road and behind the cover of the structure, they could see Cleeves and his party awaiting them. He had eleven companions by his side, the same two officers he had been with before, the rest non-commissioned men. It was an excessively large party for a duel, and that gave Craven cause for concern. He reached down to the double-barrelled pistols in the saddle holster before him and brought both locks to full cock. Paget noticed but did not react.

"You expect trouble?" he whispered.

"This many men gathered could either mean mischief, or they could attract some eyes we did not want to."

"May an apology be made to settle this matter of honour?" asked one of Cleeves' comrades.

"It is your man who is out of order here, but should he wish to retract his challenge I would not protest," replied Paget.

"Enough talk, let us fight!" Cleeves roared.

They all dismounted, and Charlie took the reins of all their horses to wait at the rear as they closed in on the cavalrymen. Cleeves already had his sabre in hand, eager to let the chaos begin. Paget unbuckled his sword belt and passed it to Craven, as one of the cavalrymen held up a sheathed sabre for him to use. Paget went forward and drew out the blade.

It was just as Craven had said it would be. The simple ward iron protected only the middle knuckles. A far cry from the double shells he normally relied on, especially against thrusts. Because he had been forewarned, the front weighting of the heavy cutting blade did not surprise him, much to the chagrin of Cleeves and his friends, who waited to mock him for being weak and feeble. Paget was anything but those things. He was of small stature, but his body was like iron, hardened through years of fighting, both in practice and against a fierce enemy.

Craven looked back from where they had travelled, half-expecting Major Spring, Thorny, or even Wellington himself to come riding in and split up the affair, but the scene was quite tranquil. Nobody was coming. It was to be a fair fight now as the two men fought with identical weapons in a duel, until the matter was considered settled to the satisfaction of the challenger, or one of them could not continue, through severe injury or death.

They took up their positions far out of measure, and Cleeves began to swing his blade about as if to intimate with his skill and speed, using the same rotations Craven had shown Paget. He clearly had been training with his weapon, but one would expect no less, for he was a cavalryman. Craven kept Paget's sword belt close in hand, with his right resting near the grip so that he might rip it from the scabbard at a moment's notice at the first sign of trouble. Although he knew Charlie would come out shooting with the pistols from their saddles if it came to it. She would not hesitate to shoot them down as if they were Frenchmen if they dared attempt to hurt Paget in any way that was outside of the strict and honourable rules of the duel.

"Gentlemen, begin!"

Both came to their guard positions stripped to their shirts, and true to form, the cavalryman carried his offhand in front and locked to his waist as if he were holding his horse's reins. Paget's offhand came up to the height of his face with the grace of a smallsword fencer, causing several of Cleeves' friends to giggle. That made Charlie's blood boil, but she would let it slide, for she was confident Paget would soon silence their mocking heckles with the skill of his sword arm.

Cleeves began the fight suddenly and hacked away with precise and powerful blows, as if he were attacking a static target to test the edge of his blade. Paget parried them away with ease and comfort, as if the blade was one he was most familiar with. For the motions were exactly as they had practiced that morning. Back and forth they clashed with quite some excitement to the level that most onlookers would assume they were of equal skill, but Paget was more relaxed and not taking certain opportunities to deliver horrifying or even fatal blows. Few would have noticed, except those who knew Paget well and had crossed blades with him in training.

Cleeves was becoming impatient as he could not strike

home no matter what he tried. So he leapt forward and swung a heavy horizontal blow as if he were cutting an infantryman's head off at full gallop in the saddle. Paget ducked under and slashed with his sword across Cleeves' body. It was a long cut that would open a vicious-looking wound, but not one that would strike so deeply as to do significant long-lasting harm. And yet as Cleeves turned back around, there was no wound where Paget's blade had slid across his torso. Something was wrong, and Craven knew it. Paget looked dumfounded before looking to his sword in disbelief.

"What the hell was that?" Ferreira asked.

"They've given him a dull blade!" Craven went to move and intervene.

"Don't," insisted Matthys.

The Sergeant's voice was enough to bring him to a halt as he knew Matthys was usually right, and he was too quick to become hot headed.

"Let him handle it and leave none in doubt of his skill."

"You would have him fight that cleaving blade with a blunt?" Ferreira asked in horror.

"He has faced far worse odds in his time here."

"He's right. He can handle himself just fine," said Craven.

The fight went on as steel clashed against steel, as Paget tried to find some answer. The point of his sword was still fine enough to go through his man, but he had promised he would not use point. He parried back and forth time and time again. Finally, one blow got through as a cut was opened on his right arm just below the shoulder. He winced with the pain but kept moving and parried the next few blows before a natural lull came in the fight, as they both caught a breath.

Cleeves was smiling maniacally as if he had already won, but Paget looked back at the blunt blade in his hands and realised he was not entirely void of offence. Just as Craven had told him, the sabres of the light cavalry carried much weight towards the tip. He had been instructed not to chop with so much force as to sever a limb, but now he had no keen edge it was of no concern, and he knew what he must do.

Cleeves came at him again, and once more he parried but gave light ripostes as he had gone through, attempting to end the affair with light drawing cuts and nothing more savage or severe. Cleeves thought he had the measure of the Lieutenant, that he had seen all he had to offer, but he had no idea how much Paget held back. It was now time for him to flip the scenario on its head.

Cleeves lashed a blow at him, and Paget parried. He thrust back with a short feint merely to provoke Cleeves, who lifted his sword in a panic to protect his face. As he went to the parry, he did not find Paget's blade. Paget rotated and let the weight carry it around behind his right shoulder before lashing down with a full motion cut and all of his might. The blunt blade struck Cleeves' sword arm with immense force, and he cried out as an audible crack rang out. His arm was broken. The sabre fell from his grasp as he collapsed to his knees and cried out in pain.

The matter was settled, and there was nothing more to be said. The cavalrymen watched on in horror as the two officers amongst them rushed to their comrade's aid. Charlie reached for Craven's double-barrelled pistol, ready to draw and come out shooting if need be, and Craven was ready to take them all, but Paget walked up to his defeated adversary without any caution at all.

"You gave me a dull blade, like you would carry on home service, but not out here," he declared loudly for all to hear.

"It must have been some mistake," protested one of Cleeves' friends.

"A cavalryman doesn't bring a dull sabre to war," he declared, as Craven came forward and took the weapon to inspect for himself. The entire edge was gleaming where it had been run over a stone and gleamed just as bright as the burrs which had been made during their battle, where the steel beneath had been exposed by chips taken from the edge as the blades clashed.

"Duelling is not well favoured by Wellington, but this, intentionally dulling the blade of your opponent in a matter of honour that you demanded! That would be an attempt to murder a fellow officer."

"I'm sorry, I…I…" stammered Cleeves as he got to his feet, cradling his lifeless arm.

"You are a disgrace to the uniform. This matter is over, and if you come after one of my own again, there will be no honourable affair. I will slit your throat whilst you sleep, do I make myself clear?"

"Yes, yes, sorry," cried Cleeves.

Craven tossed down the dull sabre in disgust before handing Paget his sword back.

"Thank you, Sir."

"Not bad," smiled Craven.

The cavalrymen said nothing more. They were humiliated and dared not make it any worse as Paget buckled his sword belt, mounted his horse, and rode away with his associates.

"I wonder what hope there is for us when the officers of

our cavalry would act with such deceit and dishonour. They are no better than the man who stole feed from his horse."

"You think too much of your countrymen. They are not all good, far from it," replied Craven.

"But they should be."

"Then do what you told them they must. Lead by example and show them the way."

"I will, I will by God!" Paget roared passionately.

CHAPTER 5

"You took a big risk letting Paget fight that man with a dull blade. He might as well have been using a singlestick against a cavalry blade," declared Ferreira as they watched Paget's triumph celebrated on returning to the Salfords.

"A sword's principal purpose is to defend oneself, and if you mean to do no harm to your adversary, then you need not have a sharp edge. Back in England the cavalry and yeomanry keep order with dull edges, but a length of steel is weapon enough when killing is not needed."

"I don't imagine they are fighting trained cavalrymen with sharp sabres, though, are they?"

"If the yeomanry are the standards that we hold ourselves to, then we are in big trouble." Matthys stepped up beside them, having been the one to restrain Craven from intervening during the duel. It was a rare scathing comment from the Sergeant, and so it cut especially deep.

"They are that bad back in England?" Ferreira asked as they thought of the cavalrymen who served only within the borders of their homeland.

"Some are better than others, but it's fair to say the standards to which they reach are not remotely comparable to our cavalry regiments."

"Many would say they merely play at soldiering. They parade through the towns in all their finery, many a man wearing a uniform better than I could ever afford. They look brave and they break hearts, but not much else," smiled Craven.

Though in truth he knew a few yeomanry regiments who were extremely capable, and yet he would still enjoy mocking them as a whole.

"It was a truly sinister thing to do to a fellow officer. That man intended to kill Paget. What a despicable man. He should count himself lucky he only suffered a broken arm, for he should be run out of the Army." Matthys was seething.

"If we kicked out every cheat and liar from this army there would be no army left," smirked Craven.

"Would you really cut that man's throat?" Ferreira asked.

"Have I ever made an empty threat?"

Ferreira shrugged.

"Though I'm not even sure I would be quick enough to get my hands on that man. You saw the way Vicenta was looking upon him with daggers in her eyes. One of us should ensure she does not go through with it before a second offence," added Craven.

"Major Craven!" roared an officer.

None of them recognised the man, though Major Spring was in the saddle beside him.

"You will present yourself to Lord Wellington immediately!"

"What is this about?"

"Ugly business. You should do as requested," insisted Spring.

The officer who made the demands did not look like a patient man, as though he would draw his sword and enforce his orders if he was made to wait any longer, and several provosts lay in wait twenty paces behind him in readiness to be called to his aid if need be.

"What is this?" Ferreira whispered.

"No idea, but it can't be good."

"I will come with you."

They fell in as Paget spotted the situation. He rushed to Matthys as Craven was led away.

"What is the meaning of this?" Paget demanded angrily.

"We do not know, but you must not meddle in whatever it is."

Paget growled with frustration.

"Is this my doing?"

"I do not believe so, for this appears far more severe," replied Matthys with deep concern.

"The Major will be all right, will he not?"

"He always finds a way," replied Matthys to calm his nerves, but the concern in his expression was there for all to see as they watched their beloved commanding officer about to be led away in a most ominous scene.

"What have you done this time?" Ferreira asked him.

"I have no idea."

"Knowing you it could be a hundred different things."

"You are no saint either," protested Craven.

"No, but I do not look for trouble. Far from it, I avoid it at all costs."

"We both know that isn't true. Maybe it was a long time ago, but not anymore. You have been right by my side through plenty of trouble."

"Yes, I have, so don't let me regret it."

Craven looked to Spring as if hoping to glean some information from him as to what they were about to face, and yet he was avoiding eye contact.

"Well, what can you tell me?" Craven demanded, as if Spring owed him a great deal, of which it was a fair to assume he did. He groaned in response, and it was clear he could say little.

"There have been grave accusations made upon you and you must answer them."

"What accusations?"

"I am not at liberty to say, but it is fair to say that you better have some good answers for them."

Craven shook his head in anger and could feel the rage building. He wanted to explode into action with sword in hand, but this was not the kind of battle he could win with strength and speed. They were led on to the house Wellington was using as his headquarters and shown into the General's office. They found him leaning back in a chair and gazing out of a window lost deep in thought.

"Major Craven, Sir." Spring took up his position behind Wellington.

He turned to face them and sighed disappointedly.

"I call for one officer and two present themselves, but

there are not two Major Cravens of the Salford Rifles, are there?"

"Sir, in the Salfords we are there for one another. That is our duty, as it should be for every soldier and his comrades," replied Ferreira.

Craven smiled as he knew it would anger Wellington.

"You may stand by your Major, as you have ridden with him and his exploits, but know that you will also fall if he does."

"Yes, Sir."

"What is this about, Sir?" Craven asked.

"I have received disturbing claims about your conduct, Major."

"From whom, Sir?"

Wellington gestured toward Spring who went to another door on the far side of the room. He opened it to let in Major Rooke, who would not make eye contact with Craven as he marched in and presented himself with great confidence and an air of arrogance.

"This snake? He has had it in for me since the day we met."

"You will hold your tongue, Sir!" Wellington cried angrily.

Craven looked as exasperated as the General, if not more so, but he could do nothing but submit as he waited to hear the crimes of which he was accused.

"Major Rooke claims you, Major Craven, were one of the principal instigators and participants in the looting which followed the taking of Ciudad Rodrigo."

Craven was lost for words as it was an outrageous claim, and he had been expecting to be accused of a crime he had indeed committed.

"A dark day that was, for it cast a great shadow over what was a great victory," added Spring.

"You cannot believe this nonsense, Sir?" pleaded Craven incredulously.

"I pray that they are not true, but Major Rooke assures me he has witnesses who can corroborate his statements."

"Who are these witnesses?"

"Men who would not show their faces or present their names for fear of violence conducted against them for doing so."

"This is complete bollocks!"

"You will restrain yourself, Craven!" Wellington shot up from his chair before he sighed and sat down once more.

"I would not attack a man for making an allegation against me, Sir!"

"And yet this very afternoon you participated in a duel over such a provocation, did you not?" replied Rooke.

"Did you hear that from the same men who make these ridiculous looting accusations? Those bastards would hold a grudge and say anything to mark my name."

But it was too late. The damage was done. Wellington's eyebrow raised at this new piece of information which he was clearly not privy to previously.

"Well?"

Craven sighed, knowing Rooke had him by the balls, as Wellington was furious with the officers of his army who continued to duel over petty issues whilst there was a war to be fought. Craven could not deny it, and in doing so lost all credibility in denying the more severe offences. Rooke had chosen his timing to reveal each piece of information with supreme skill, as if he was as good a lawyer as Craven was a swordsman.

"Well, Major, do you deny this accusation also?" Wellington demanded.

"I do not, Sir, but I must explain for there is a lot more to this story."

"I expressively forbid you from duelling, Craven."

"I did not take any part of it, Sir."

"You were not Lieutenant Paget's second?" Rooke questioned him.

Wellington's eyebrow rose once more.

"Not only did you oversee and partake in this affair, but you let Paget do something so stupid?"

"He was right to do so, Sir, for he did make the challenge. His opponent even cheated and provided a dull blade, a most heinous crime."

But he had lost the respect and trust of Wellington already and was digging himself a greater hole. The circumstances seemed absurd, as it sounded like he was desperately clawing at his accusers with the most ridiculous of stories. He said no more, knowing it would do him no good. He was not guilty of the charges Rooke had brought before him, and so either the Major was lying, or those who had come forward as witnesses were. Either way, the truth of the duel earlier that day firmly painted Craven as guilty, and he had no idea how to explain his way out of it.

"Sir, I promise you the Major did not do these crimes," insisted Ferreira.

"I wish I could believe you, Captain, but how can I? You are one of the Major's closest friends. You would say and do anything to protect him, and I can respect that."

"The Major must be charged and run out of the King's Army," insisted Rooke.

Wellington sighed. That was the last thing he wanted. He could not afford to lose soldiers, let alone one as capable as Craven.

"Let us go through this again. For I will not make any decision without all of the facts which are available to us."

* * *

"What do you think he has done this time?" Charlie asked Paget.

"I don't know, but it cannot be good. You saw the expression on Major Spring's face. This must be severe."

Most of the Salfords were sitting about idle, deep in concern for their leader and friend. Hawkshaw was alone once more as he looked out into the distance in a melancholic state, not interacting with anyone.

"I can't help but think this is about my actions," Paget sounded worried.

"If it were, then you would have been hauled up there with Craven, if not before him."

He knew she was right, but his right leg tapped up and down with a nervous twitch. He desperately wanted to know more. He caught sight of several riders approaching and launched to his feet with anticipation. It was not Craven, but it was a familiar face. His heart sank, for it was Timmerman, and even though they had buried the hatchet, he was still never comfortable around the man who had tried to kill him on more than one occasion. He looked in good spirits as he rode up and stopped before them.

"Where is Craven?" he asked enthusiastically.

"He was marched to Lord Wellington."

"Marched? What has he done this time?" Timmerman smiled.

"Nobody knows, but it appears it is quite severe," fretted Paget.

"How severe?" Timmerman asked more seriously.

"The provosts were sent to collect our Major."

"Provosts? Nothing good ever involves those parasites." He looked around as if expecting trouble to find him also.

"I think Craven might be in the worst of spots, Sir," declared Paget as if to plead for help to the most unlikely of people, making it quite clear just how desperate he really was.

"Well, what are you going to do about it?"

"There is nothing we can do." Paget knew as a lowly Lieutenant he was powerless.

"You have fought beside Craven in battle after battle, but this is where you draw the line?"

Paget shrugged, realising he feared Wellington more than the French.

"Well, then, I suppose if nobody will speak for him, then I will." Timmerman turned his horse about and galloped away.

"Wait!" Paget feared he had set a terrible set of events in motion, as if he had released a bloodhound to go after Craven.

"Leave him be. There is nothing you can say to stop him anyway," insisted Matthys.

"But Timmerman will wreak havoc."

"Exactly. Whatever trouble Craven finds himself

embroiled in that man will ride through like a squadron of heavy cavalry," smiled Matthys.

"But Timmerman is a madman."

"What good are our sensibilities now? I say let him make the charge, not that you can hold him back, for he is as ill-disciplined as the heavies also, and every bit as dangerous."

Paget watched Timmerman tear off into the distance imagining what chaos would ensue.

"I truly hope you are right."

They were still in the dark as to what troubles Craven faced, and yet they all knew they must be grave.

* * *

"Sir, I did not loot, and where was the Major when we were clawing our way through the breach, fighting for every inch with cold steel and taking this city, paid for in our blood? Where was he?" Craven desperately tried to defend his honour in the face of exceptional charges.

Wellington looked deeply conflicted. He wanted to believe Craven, and yet he knew he was quite capable of doing great mischief, and the evidence against him was rather compelling. The room fell silent as he considered his next step. He knew a court martial should follow, and Rooke had made it clear in no uncertain terms that he demanded it several times over. Yet Wellington looked for any means to resolve the scenario in a different manner, for the process was exhausting at a time when there was so much to be done. He did not want to see Craven fall, for he was just the sort of reckless but capable fighter they needed in the new campaign in Spain.

He got up and paced back and forth, sighing as he struggled to find some solution. Yet the facts were the facts, and it seemed impossible for them to be brushed aside. Major Rooke was standing firm and demanding an answer. Wellington had ensured he had a reputation as a firm if fair disciplinarian, and so he could not step back now. He could not make an exception for one officer, especially as Rooke would surely make certain the entire Army knew he had done so. He finally stopped, and with one last pained gasp opened his mouth to speak and give his final words on the matter as overall Commander of the army in Portugal and Spain. Before he could get a word out the doors to his makeshift office burst open, and Timmerman came crashing through them with two men in pursuit who dared not lay a hand upon him.

"What is the meaning of this?"

He did not even seem angry, which was most curious as he had a famously short temper and would not accept such a rude entrance from anyone but a messenger with the most important of news. And yet he had clung onto the hope of some way to see Craven free and clear of the charges brought against him, and this seemed the very last chance he had.

"Sir, you have no business here," insisted Rooke.

"I will be the judge of that," sneered Timmerman.

Rooke looked most put out but also a little intimidated. Timmerman carried himself with such confidence and aggression, like a hungry wolf.

"An accusation has been made against Craven?" he asked Wellington.

"There has. Major Rooke here insists that Major Craven

was at the forefront of the looting following the assault on Ciudad Rodrigo, and that he has witnesses who will testify as such."

"That is curious." He looked to Craven and then Rooke as he tried to understand what was going on.

Craven looked lost, as if Timmerman had arrived to drive the final nail into his coffin, and he was entirely powerless now. For this was not a fight he could win with either his fencing prowess or his quick tongue.

"Curious, how?" Wellington probed, looking for any spark of hope to see an end to the unfortunate situation.

"For I was by Major Craven's side after the assault on the fortress, and I can confirm beyond all doubt that he played no part in any looting."

He looked to Craven and came out in complete support.

"And who are you to question the evidence I have brought before this hearing?" Rooke demanded.

Timmerman paused and smiled before slowly pacing across the room to the Major. Every heavy step of his boots echoed throughout the room before he stopped uncomfortably close to Rooke and got the measure of the man.

"I am Major Sir Alexander Vandertray Timmerman, and I give my word as a gentleman that Major Craven did not loot, nor did he incite others to do so. Any man who says otherwise is a liar and will answer to me."

Rooke stumbled back a few paces and began to stammer as he tried to appeal to Wellington.

"General, Sir, I…I have…" he began.

But Wellington was quick to interrupt him.

"Major Rooke. Timmerman is no friend of Major Craven,

in fact quite the opposite. For their history is well known, and so I can see no reason to not trust this statement. Craven has the support of this witness, and no court will see any reason to doubt this claim. Whilst I am sure you brought this matter to our attention with the best of intentions, the witnesses who came before you must have been confused."

"Confused?"

"Major Timmerman knows Craven well and confirms beyond all doubt that he was there and can confirm no wrongdoing, or would you call into dispute his honour?"

Rooke looked back to Timmerman who smirked back, as if begging him to do so. He would be quite within his rights to demand satisfaction from a fellow officer who would have to call him a liar to continue to pursue the case against Craven. He soon shied away as Timmerman was a frightful figure who had quite the reputation. And being in his presence was even more intimidating than the notorious figure he had cut would even suggest.

"Well?" Wellington asked.

Rooke shook his head.

"Good." Wellington slammed his hand triumphantly on his desk, "Now let us all get on with this war, shall we, gentlemen?"

They made a quick toast to the King before leaving with Rooke seething, but Craven grabbed him by the arm and stopped him from fleeing before he could say a few words.

"What do you want?" Rooke snapped as he was forced to turn and face him.

"I have no reason to lie, for I face no charges. There was no looting on my part or any of the Salford Rifles. Timmerman was right about that, and I give you my word on that."

"And why would I believe it?" Rooke hissed.

"I don't know if you were given false information or if you fabricated this against me, but I did not loot, and if you continue to come after me, it will not end well for you," threatened Craven.

"You are a disgrace the uniform, and you will get what's coming to you." Rooke snatched his arm away and stormed off.

"How can you let him talk to you that way?" Timmerman asked.

"I have just narrowly escaped a court martial. How would it look if I tried to kill the man who brought charges against me?"

"Like justice, like revenge," smiled Timmerman as he delighted in the prospect.

"Exactly."

"He got you out of a whole world of pain." Ferreira looked to Timmerman in amazement.

"Yes, he did," admitted Craven who was glad of the surprise as he looked to his old adversary and tried to understand why he would step in to help.

"I don't hate you, Craven, not anymore, for we have long since had our dance, or many dances," he smirked as he reminisced over their great clashes with sword in hand.

"We avoid men we tolerate. We do not go to their aid."

"You and me, we were born to fight. Born with a blade in our hands, and we were born into the very best of times. We are warriors and there is a war to fight. What a tragedy it would be to rob this war of such a warrior."

Craven looked impressed, and yet he knew there must be

more to the story.

"You couldn't have known about these charges. You came looking for me for another purpose, didn't you?"

"Well, yes."

"I see how it is. You need something from me?"

"More I have an opportunity for you," smiled Timmerman with a devilishly mysterious smile.

CRAVEN'S WAR – THE FINAL CHANCE

CHAPTER 6

"That is your plan?" Ferreira asked in disbelief as the officers of the Salford Rifles gathered around to hear what Timmerman had to say. At the centre of the table was a map of the area that they had all been studying carefully.

"What do you think?" Timmerman asked Craven.

"We are here to fight a war, not to hunt for treasure," insisted Paget who looked most unimpressed by the concept.

"Spoken like a man who is already wealthy, but you are not anymore, are you?" replied Craven.

Paget shrugged, as it was indeed true.

"Most men put on this uniform for pay and nothing more, but we aren't paid enough, not any of us, and when this war finally ends there will be a great many men without any work at all."

"What are you saying, Sir?"

"That a large standing army is no longer required once the

threat of Napoleon is no more," replied Ferreira.

"Especially in England, for when this war is over, we will once more rely on the Royal Navy for the safety of our great country, and the Army will be reduced many times over," Craven added.

"I won't be a part of this," insisted Hawkshaw, and he left the room.

But Paget stayed, for unlike Hawkshaw, he did not have a home and a great deal of money to return to.

"I didn't imagine I'd ever have to steal to make my way," admitted Paget.

"It isn't stealing when you take from the enemy. It is plunder, and it is fair game. I can bet you a sizeable sum that your father and his before him are living off plunder from their forefathers."

"Except you don't have a sizeable sum to gamble, Sir," smiled Paget.

"Neither do you. Not yet anyway."

"So, in short, Marshal Soult is sending great riches from Cadiz back to France, and you want to steal them from him?" Ferreira asked.

"Exactly so."

"And why involve us?"

"Because you have all the luck in the world, Craven, and because as much as I always hated you for it, you are a mighty fine soldier. When you set yourself to something it invariably gets done."

"And you don't want to fail and be dragged to France to live out this war as a prisoner?"

"That, too."

"Why not wait until Badajoz is taken?" Paget asked.

"Because if we succeed in taking the city, then Soult will flee with all haste, and we will never have a chance at any of his riches, for they will be long outside of our reach."

"Even when we march into France and on to Paris?"

"We don't know what could happen then. A peace could be signed, and we might never have another chance again, but out here on the frontier, French supply wagons go missing every day as the guerrillas make their attacks, let alone our own boys," replied Timmerman.

"But why now?" Ferreira asked.

"Because the army is about to march, and with that momentum will come chaos, and because I know when Soult's wagons will be on the road."

"How can you know any of that?" Paget asked.

"Rumour has it we will not move on Badajoz for many more weeks," added Craven.

"That is what everyone believes, including the French, which is why Wellington will do the opposite, just as he did on the first day of the year. He had the army march through snowstorms so that they might gain the element of surprise."

"We know, we were there," groaned Paget.

"In all that chaos we might just pull this off."

"And you are sure the army is about to march?"

They could hear a commotion outside as riders galloped on by yelling enthusiastically. Ferreira rushed to the door and peered out for himself.

"He's right. The army is to march for Badajoz," replied Craven.

They were painfully aware of how formidable Badajoz

was, as they had already failed to take it the previous year. It was a much stronger fortification than Ciudad Rodrigo, and it would be defended by a far larger force of French troops.

"Should we not march with the army, Sir?"

"Our role is to be out ahead of them, scouting and causing chaos. This idea of Timmerman's seems to be precisely that."

"But we will surely be needed at Badajoz," insisted Paget.

"Indeed, but it will be weeks before this army can reach the city," added Timmerman.

"What do you say, Sir?" Paget asked Craven as he would never presume to push for something the Major did not agree to.

"If we can get our hands on those riches, then we should."

"A great deal of that wealth was taken from my people," declared Vicenta who came out from the shadows of another room nearby.

"What would you have us do?" Craven asked.

"Anything of great importance to my people should be returned to them, and Francisco De Rosas always needs help. You owe him. Give some share to his cause, a quarter of the wealth."

"That would satisfy you?"

"Many of the people whose money was taken are no longer alive to have it returned, and I would see those who go on risking everything to see some reward, yes."

"Word of this could never reach Wellington. Nobody could know we were ever involved."

"That should not be a problem," declared Timmerman.

Craven looked about the room to see that everyone was in agreement.

"Then let us be on our way and make our fortune!"

A cheer rang out, and Craven made his way for the door to find Major Spring approaching.

"Shit," muttered Craven.

The last time he came looking for them it was to bring bad news and ignite a fire beneath his feet. He and the rest of them filed outside to hear what news the Major brought.

"Don't look so worried, Major, for you are a free man with your honour intact."

"What is it, then?" demanded Craven suspiciously.

"Badajoz is in our sights now."

"And you would have us scout ahead of the army?" asked Craven as if it would come as no surprise at all.

"Actually, no. Wellington is concerned that Badajoz will be a far bloodier affair than Rodrigo. A bitter contest at close quarters with sword and bayonet."

"How could it not?"

"Quite. Well, it so happens that you are most talented in these matters, a great prize fighter who has been slugging his entire life," declared Spring as if to lay down praise to butter him up before making his demands, or in this case, providing orders.

"What do you want?" Craven groaned.

"Wellington wants to give our boys the best fighting chance when they get to the walls of Badajoz, and hopefully up and over them. He wants you to march with the army, and every evening at rest you will instruct some officers and sergeants of many different regiments. You will share your knowledge and turn those men into lions so that they may in turn teach those under their command to do the same."

"Now? In the days and weeks leading up to a siege? This

should have been done back in England and long before ever facing the enemy."

"You sound like General Le Marchant, for he is quite the school master and would have us all learning from books about every subject pertaining to the duties of a soldier."

"He is right, particularly in the case of the sword and bayonet. Men cannot learn all they need to know in a few evenings of teaching, let alone when they are tired from a long march."

"I am sure you are right, but whilst you may not have the time to bestow all that you know upon these men, you may well improve their skills beyond their current level, don't you think? Or do you not believe a few lessons from yourself can make a difference to a man's fighting ability?"

"Of course, they can," replied Craven defensively.

Spring smiled, knowing he had caused Craven to fall upon his own sword by appealing to his self-belief and confidence in his fighting qualities, as well as his well-known ability to impart those skills upon others.

"For the next few weeks, you are to be drill master, Major. You will make our soldiers twice as fearsome in close quarters."

"I hear the French attach a fencing master to every regiment."

"It's true," added Timmerman.

"Well perhaps this will be the start," replied Spring before leaving as quickly as he had arrived.

"There goes your plan," muttered Craven.

"Our plan, and no, far from it. We will travel with the army and instruct them along the way. We will bide our time until the right moment. We have a little over two weeks until we must intercept the Marshal's wagons."

"Must?"

"Do you want to be poor all your life?"

Craven shook his head, but the concept made him curious.

"And you? Why are you doing this? You have never wanted for riches."

"That is where you are wrong. A man lives to his means. I can spend money quicker than Napoleon can march across Europe," he smiled.

"Craven laughed as it was as absurd as it was entirely plausible, considering everything he knew about his old adversary.

"The French Marshals make themselves rich off of this war, and Soult is one of the very worse of them, but we will take our share, and we will keep on taking from them until the day this war is over."

"And then?"

"We will find new ways to take from them!" he laughed, "Do you know that before the war it was commonplace for cocky French swordsmen to wait around at bars and cafes in coastal towns and in Paris, eager to cause insult and encourage a challenge, only to demand to fight with swords. Of course, most Englishmen have long since duelled with pistols and are quite ignorant of the sword. Imagine in peace time if we visited such places and what could be achieved."

"By duelling?" Paget asked in amazement.

"Do you know what sort of money those sorts of men are willing to wager?"

That made Paget most uncomfortable, but gambling was what led Craven into trouble countless times, even just in the time they had known one another. There was an almighty clatter of equipment as non-commissioned officers stormed about barking their orders, and the troops billeted all around them sprang to life. Some had been living in local residences whilst others were less lucky to be under canvas, though many counted themselves fortunate. Sleeping under the stars was not uncommon due to the shortages, and tents were one of the very last pieces of equipment to arrive for the army.

"Do you really mean to ride with us and teach the army alongside us?" Craven asked Timmerman.

"Absolutely, fresh meat, we will have some fun along the way."

"Not a word to anyone about our plans regarding Soult's wagons, do you hear me?"

"Of course, I would not want to share that treasure with the whole army!"

Timmerman strode away to make his preparations to march on with the army. Craven was still smiling as much in surprise for the events unfolding before them, but he soon noticed Paget looking deeply conflicted.

"What is it? Still bothered by the prospect of stealing?"

"No, Sir. Taking riches from the enemy is quite all right, but Timmerman would not share it with all of our regiment?"

Craven shrugged as it was true that the Salford Rifles had grown into a formidable outfit of several hundred soldiers.

"If we do this, then it will be a handful of us who make the attempt. Only those few will take the risks and also benefit from the rewards should we be successful."

But Paget was not comforted by that fact.

"You would have us share with the entire regiment?"

"They have been there for us throughout, Sir. The only reason we are able to chance such a daring thing is because of them."

"You would have us bring every man up with us? Careful Mr Paget, for that sounds like revolutionary speak!" Craven laughed.

Paget did not see the funny side, and Craven was impressed to see the changes he had made. He had been a spoilt boy with little understanding of the common soldier's woes, but not anymore. Now he appeared to care.

"Has involuntary poverty given you some perspective?"

"Amongst other things, yes. I would see every soldier who serves under us benefit when we do."

"Then they will, for it is the right thing to do."

"When have you ever cared about that, Sir?" replied Paget in a biting fashion.

"I could say the same about you and about the plight of the common soldier."

"War will make men of us all. That is what my father used to tell me. He was right, but not in the way that he meant."

"You really care what happens to them all, don't you?"

"I do, Sir, and I should want the best for every man who serves with us after all of this is over. Bringing an end to this war and freeing these lands from Napoleon is of great importance, but afterwards we would all want to live a good life."

"And after it, what would you have us do?"

"For many of our Portuguese friends they will return home, hopefully richer than they left, but for the rest of us, we must find a way for the Salford Rifles to live on."

"How could they? We only exist to fight this war, and

when it is done so shall we be. The British Army is mobilised into the greatest fighting force it has ever been, but when the threat of Napoleon is gone, we will not be needed."

"Then we must find a way to stay relevant. For we possess such great qualities that must not be wasted, and we have created a family which must stay together."

Craven nodded in appreciation as he felt the same. He had known comradery in the past in the early years of his military career and especially as a prize fighter, but none of that came close to the bounds they had forged with the Salford Rifles.

"We will find a way, won't we, Sir?" pressed Paget as he dreamed of the future.

"We surely will, but those days are so far in the distance they are nothing but dreams for now. This war will not end this year or next, and that is what we should concern ourselves with for now. If we cannot get through these years, there will be nothing to concern ourselves with in the future."

Matthys stormed up before them.

"The order is here. The army is to march."

"Yes, they are, and Wellington would have us not just march with the army but instruct it in the use of the sword and bayonet when we make camp each day."

Matthys could not look more overjoyed by the prospect, as it meant they would stay within the safety of the army.

"Major Craven, sword master to the Army," he smiled.

"Was that not the very reason we came out here?" he replied, as he thought back to when he had been recruited to help with the training of Portuguese troops.

"That was what you said we would be doing. This time we'll actually be doing it."

"You have nothing to fear, Sir, for you are an excellent teacher," insisted Paget.

But Craven groaned as it was not what he wanted for himself.

"Perhaps a path for the future, Sir, the Salford School of Fencing?" he declared enthusiastically.

The grimace left his face as the concept sounded rather good, but he caught Matthys enjoying the moment.

"Prepare to move. We will not be returning, not unless we fail."

Matthys bellowed his orders for all to hear as they prepared to vacate the lodgings that had kept them quite cosily for a little while, both before and after the successful assault of the fortress. Spring was still several weeks away, and nobody was keen to march on through the winter, but the threat of the French armies in Spain coming to oppose them was reason enough to light a fire beneath them and keep them going forward.

The entire area sprang to life as the troops prepared to move onwards, and soon enough they were all on the road South. It was a little over one hundred and fifty miles to Badajoz as they marched along the border just within the security of the Portuguese territory. It was not a great distance for a small, mounted troop, but for an army of tens of thousands it was a monstrous logistical nightmare that would take weeks. As a result, it was a slow and meandering journey, but also a rather relaxed one, unlike so many of the desperate and time sensitive missions they had conducted in the past. With the vast army in front and behind, they felt remarkably safe as they were able to let their guard down and enjoy the journey. It was as if it were merely a leisurely journey through a peaceful England, and not a war-torn nation with armies of tens of thousands of Frenchmen waiting to pounce upon them.

The army did not march until sunset or even a little into the night as Craven would often insist. For it was a great deal of work to prepare an army to make camp and also break it.

"At least we shall fence in the light, for I had visions of us practicing by the light of our campfire, and it would not be the first time!" Paget roared excitedly as they stopped for the day.

Indeed, he was right. The men and animals needed to be fed and provided for. Pickets needed to be set and tents erected. It was a great deal of fanfare for a single night before setting off on the road the next day. So much so that when the first class of students arrived the sun was already very low in the sky and the campfires raging. He had been sent twelve sergeants and a single officer. A modest party to teach, and he was glad of that fact. He could focus his time on their development, though none of them looked eager to be there, and he couldn't blame them. They had been on the march all day. They remained quite relaxed and casual, and none had reported to him as they had surely been ordered. Craven smiled as he imagined just how furious he would be in their shoes.

"My name is Major Craven, and I am here to show you how to fight," he declared, knowing it would raise more than a few eyebrows.

"Have we not been fighting all this time?" jeered one of the sergeants, gaining laughter from the rest.

"You have been fighting no doubt, but how well?"

"Well enough," came the reply.

Craven smiled and laughed along with them.

"Rodrigo was a fine victory, but Badajoz, well Badajoz will be ten times the battle. I can assure you of that, for I have seen its walls, and we have tried to take that damned place and failed. But we cannot fail a second time. Fail a second time and this whole damned war could be lost."

"We know that. We can fight, we have been fighting," insisted the same Sergeant who had spoken up before.

He was in his late twenties and certainly held himself with confidence and experience, and his face was marked from several old wounds. He looked strong despite his fairly narrow frame, the sort of strength one builds working as a farmhand. His black hair had already started to grey in places. He had lived a hard life but carried a lot of pride on his shoulders.

"Many a man who joins this army knew how to fight long before he ever put on a uniform. I count myself amongst them, but I assure you there is always room for improvement. But I can see you are practical and honest men who would like proof and not just words, is that correct?"

"It is!" roared the Sergeant.

Craven smiled as he had reeled in the man just as he wanted.

"Fix your bayonet," ordered Craven.

The Sergeant looked surprised but also a little excited as he imagined he might get a chance to prove himself. He began to unfix his sheathed bayonet by prising the frog stud out of the leather hanger where it hung at his belt.

"Don't worry about all that. I want you to fix cold steel, bare for us all to see."

The Sergeant looked surprised, but he did not question it as he drew out the hollow ground triangular section socket bayonet. It glimmered against the last rays of sunlight. The socket bayonet for the Land Pattern Musket was only for thrusting. It looked more like a robust smallsword blade than the edged sword type blade used upon rifles. Despite lacking any cutting capability, it was far stiffer and more robust, and could deal horrifically broad wounds compared to the sword bayonet. It would not bend out of shape due to its rigid structural profile.

"Step forward!"

The Sergeant stepped out of the loosely gathered party as Craven went to a pile of equipment. He unhooked his sword belt and laid it down before taking up a singlestick and returning to them. The small class could barely believe what they were seeing, not imagining for a moment that he would fight against the bare steel with a stick. The crowd watching knew better and watched with glee as the situation unfolded before their very eyes. Several of the sergeants who were now students began to chuckle as if Craven had made a grave mistake.

"Lord Wellington would have every man who goes before the enemy to be the very best he can be with sword and bayonet. Much of this war is decided with cannon, musket, and rifle, but after all is said and done, it is with cold steel that many affairs are decided. Many men will run at the sight of a bayonet charge, but those who stand may hold and throw you back. Wellington wants me to ensure you have the best chance of defeating the enemy when that time comes!"

"It's a bayonet. We know how to use it," insisted the Sergeant who awaited him with fixed bayonet.

"What is your name, Sergeant?"

"Griffiths, Sir."

"Well, Sergeant Griffiths, do you believe the musket and

bayonet has advantage over the sword?"

"Yes, Sir."

"Why?"

"It is longer, heavier, stronger, and I can hit you from farther away."

"Prove it."

Griffiths looked a little uncomfortable.

"These are your orders."

"Sir, I cannot attempt to strike an officer."

"That is not your role. I am ordering you to conduct this exercise. Should you harm me in any way, then you have countless witnesses to prove it was misadventure on my part, and you will not be held to blame. You will try and kill me. Do you understand me?"

Still the Sergeant looked hesitant.

"Is this how you act before the enemy? Do you hesitate, Sergeant? Do you question your orders? Do you quake in fear and look to others to do your job, Sergeant!"

He had pushed all the right buttons. Griffiths was now shaking with anger as he cried out with a loud battle cry and levelled the musket and bayonet at Craven. He darted forward with murderous intent, charging and thrusting with the bayonet with enough force to skewer a boar. Yet Craven nimbly parried with his singlestick. He locked his blade into the elbow of the bayonet where it protruded from the rifle to give enough space to use the ramrod. He pushed it aside and took hold of the musket with his left and closed the distance, presenting the point of his singlestick to the man's chest as if to run a sword through his heart. Griffiths was stunned, and in that moment had caught the attention of all who had come to be taught by him. They watched wide-eyed and in disbelief as a man with a stick overcame an experienced soldier with musket and bayonet. Craven released his grasp from Griffiths' weapon and stepped away.

"Would you like to know how you could win that fight, whether in your shoes or mine?"

"Yes, Sir, please show us the way," he replied enthusiastically as he went back to the others and complained no further as Craven addressed them.

"I will teach you to be better than you are but know this. To teach you well would require six weeks, practicing six hours a day for six days of every week. That is what I would like to give you, but we do not have this time. I will do everything I can in the time that we have together, that is my promise to you. All I ask is that you submit to my teachings so that we do not waste a single minute. Can you do that for me?"

"Yes, Sir!" they roared enthusiastically.

CHAPTER 7

Every day was the same as they rode on at a leisurely pace through the beautiful countryside, and by evening practiced with sword and bayonet with a different body of soldiers well after the sun had gone down. On the second night the new body of men were just as doubtful of Craven's teachings and their need of them as the first had been. Once again, he made a great show to win them over. The third day of marching was coming to a close as Craven sat down to rest, not expecting to have to conduct the training until near dark when the men had fully prepared the camp.

"Major Craven, Sir?"

He looked up to see the men who had been assigned to him that evening had already arrived, early and eager, and more than double the number he would have expected. He shot up in surprise as if expecting some kind of trouble.

"What are you doing here?"

"Sir, we heard what you are doing for the others. We want to learn what they have learnt," declared a Captain, one of three officers who had come to attend the class.

Craven was stunned. It was not common for a soldier to volunteer to do work, least of all after a long day on the march, and yet they arrived with the sort of eagerness Paget regularly exhibited, which was a rare sight indeed. The enthusiastic officer went on as Craven remained in a stunned silence.

"When we climb the walls of Badajoz, Sir, we want to deal such a blow to the French they will never forget. Every one of us can fight, we have proven that, but I believe you can make us better than we have ever been. Is that true, Sir?"

Craven coughed as he cleared his dry throat. He had been caught completely off guard and yet it was a pleasant surprise.

"One thing I can say for certain is that no matter your skill or experience, you can always become better than you are, and we must never stop learning. I cannot make you into something completely different in a few hours, but I can make you better than you were this morning or yesterday. That much I guarantee."

They all looked eager to begin, and a far cry from the previous two groups who looked entirely despondent upon presenting themselves for instruction. Yet it was a far larger group than he'd want to handle. He looked back his camp and could see Timmerman watching on with curiosity. They now made camp together, which still felt strange after all they had been through.

"Well? Will you lend a hand in teaching these fine men?"

"Me?" he asked with a smile as he approached.

"This is Major Timmerman, a real cold bastard, and just

the sort of man you want standing beside you when you find yourself surrounded by Frenchmen!"

He drew a great amount of laughter, including from Timmerman himself, who nodded in appreciation of the sentiment. It was the greatest compliment he had ever received from Craven as they finally understood one another. He took up position beside Craven as Paget joined them as Craven's regular assistant. The crowd was silent. There were no groans nor whispers amongst naysayers and doubters. The soldiers who had come to be taught took it as seriously as those who had paid a great deal of money to learn from a teacher in their own private time.

"The Army teaches you to march with musket and bayonet. How to direct it in a charge, and nothing more, leaving each man to his own devices to fight with musket and bayonet as if were a drunken brawl. Each man reliant on his own skills and strengths. This is foolish, and one day I hope those in charge see differently. Do you think the Roman legions only learnt to march and throw spears? Do you believe they left it to each man to develop his own style of spear and swordsmanship? No, I can assure you they did not, because the use of the sword and bayonet is not some senseless brawl, or it should not be. It is an art and a science. Art regulates nature, and with instruction and guidance can lead us to the true science of defence. For that is what fighting is, first and foremost, the art of defence. This science must be taught and understood, and once it is understood, it must be practiced like anything you wish to master. Practice, more so than science and theory conserves and improves our skills. What does all of this mean you may ask? It means you need to learn better ways to fight, and then you need to practice them regularly. I can give the former, but the latter is down to you. When you have some down time, when you are restless in barracks, when you sit idle, will you choose to practice? I can assure you the French do. We Englishmen have become too reliant in close quarters on our brutishness, but in this simplicity, you will find your limitations."

"That's enough talk. Let's get fighting," insisted Timmerman.

"Quite so," agreed Craven.

Craven opened his mouth again to ask for the same challenge he had done so the previous two days when he stopped himself, realising these men were not just there because they had been ordered to. They had been told what the practice entailed. He went and picked up a wooden pole with a padded canvas cover over one end, a simple training tool to allow them to practice bayonet combat against one another and against the singlesticks.

"This is my musket and bayonet, who believes the bayonet has an advantage over the sword?"

Many hands went up.

"Why?"

"It's longer!" roared one of them.

"Okay, in simple terms you are correct. Let us accept that for now, the bayonet has the advantage. What if there are two swordsmen against one bayonet, then do they gain the advantage?"

There were grumbles in agreement and not a single one against, and so Craven grabbed two singlesticks and tossed them onto the ground before his new students.

"Two volunteers to face me. Come forward."

It was two of the officers who leapt at the chance. For they were most accustomed to the use of the sword and believed they were in with a chance and eager to prove themselves. They picked up the singlesticks as Craven backed away into a wide-open space where they could conduct their experiment. Two against one seemed like an obvious and large advantage, and any soldier who had fought in combat or even in practice knew that to be true. They approached him with their swords extended in guard as the crowd watched with much anticipation. Craven thrust towards one, but as the man reacted, Craven twisted a little and drove his padded stick into the flank of the other who did not have any time to react at all. He looked stunned to be hit before he could even respond. The other man lowered his sword as if to give up.

"You are not done yet, or would you lay down your weapon before the enemy?" Craven taunted him.

Once again, the officer took up his guard. Craven lifted his bayonet, directed it well above his opponent's head so that it could not be engaged with the sword. He struck down as if to cut, despite their bayonets not having any edges, but he was not striking for the man, but the sword in his hands. The padded stick battered through the sword and created a great opening with which Craven drove home with a thrust to the chest. The crowd were stunned but soon began to clap with appreciation for the swift display. There was little doubt in their minds before, but now they had absolute confidence in the skills of the men they had come to learn from. They clung onto Craven's every word as he went on.

"There is a lot to know about fighting with the sword and bayonet, but principally there are a few things which the army should be teaching you, but they do not. Firstly, the musket and bayonet is a clumsy weapon if you do not use it efficiently, and the sword is weak against the bayonet if that too is not used correctly. What do I mean by this? A musket is heavy, awkward and slow, but if you do not know how to fight against it, then it can have all the qualities of the Sergeant's spontoon. A spear, a most formidable weapon which man has used for thousands of years. Use feints, deceptions, and only use the mass of the weapon when it is safe to do so. Let's get started!"

They began their training, which went on long after dark as the troops eagerly soaked up all the knowledge and practice they could. Major Spring approached as they continued on with sparring games with only the distant light of fires and the moon to guide them. He stepped up beside Craven who was overseeing the games as Timmerman and Paget actively participated, pushing the volunteers to their limits and giving coached sparring.

"You have caused quite a stir. It seems everywhere I go I hear about Craven and his classes on how to fight. Go on like this, and you might become a reformer yourself, just like Le Marchant."

"You think the army would make a manual of swordsmanship and bayonet fencing on foot?"

"Because of you? No. General Le Marchant did not have his cavalry exercise accepted amongst the army because it was what was best for the army, but because he has friends in the right places."

"He has the ear of King George, does he not?"

"And a great many others, indeed, and the wealth to run with such royalty."

"I have no wealth and no friends in high places," sighed Craven.

"You do not count Lord Wellington?" Spring asked in surprise.

"He has no love of me," Craven chuckled.

"That is where you are wrong."

"Come on, Major. Wellington tolerates us because I am useful, but nothing more."

"No, you are wrong."

"You have seen how flustered he gets."

"Yes, I have, but I have also seen the joy and relief upon your successes. Lord Wellington will not forget what you have done for him and for England. Pay his temper no attention, for he is no different with his closest friends."

Craven appreciated the sentiment but was surprised to hear it.

"I think he assigned you this task to keep you out of trouble and close on hand. I don't for a minute believe he thought the men would see some merit in it and volunteer for these extra duties."

"To be good at something you must practice, and to learn that thing you must have a teacher who knows his subject. How is this still a surprise to anybody?"

Craven was angry and frustrated at how little attention was given to the sword and bayonet use.

"Sometimes we do not do the things we should because we never knew we needed to."

Craven smiled and nodded in agreement. In the morning they were on the road once more with the same routine they had come to expect. The journey and the evenings exercises were a welcome distraction from the formidable and daunting task which lay ahead. Nobody was under any illusions about what Badajoz would be like. They had all lived and fought through the assault on a fortress, and in many ways that made it worse, for they knew how bad it was going to get. Yet a little before noon the routine was broken as Major Spring came galloping towards them with great urgency. He drew to a halt very abruptly and had a worried-looking private of the light horse beside him.

"What is it?" Craven asked.

"A troop of cavalry scouts has been caught out by French cavalry. They have lost most of their horses and are trapped."

"Where?"

"Five miles East."

"What is the enemy strength?"

"Unknown."

Craven looked back and forth to see there was no other cavalry in sight, and those of the Salfords who possessed horses were the closest to such a force.

"Everyone in the saddle. On me, now!"

Thirty riders were all they could muster, which included every officer of the regiment.

"Jenkins here will lead you to them. He is one of theirs."

"I'm afraid my horse is shot, Sir, for it was a hard ride to reach you," replied Jenkins.

He was a young man of Paget's stature and with boyish features, and yet the confidence of an experienced veteran.

"Take mine." Spring dismounted and exchanged mounts with the Private but did not mount the exhausted animal.

"Lead the way!" Craven ordered.

They left at a canter, knowing they could not risk fatiguing their horses too quickly.

"How many are you?" Craven rode beside Jenkins.

"We were forty-six, Sir."

It was a modest force, but the Anglo Portuguese army never had enough cavalrymen, and every single man and horse would be needed for the ongoing campaign.

"And the enemy?"

"I am not certain, Sir."

"Why would they attack so close to the army as it marches, Sir?" Paget had come up beside them.

"To slow us down. They will do anything to slow our advance, just as we have done to them."

"How can they know we move on Badajoz after just several days of the march?"

"They must have known it was a possibility no matter how unlikely they thought it."

"I do hope there are still survivors," sobbed Jenkins.

"For them as much as us. For if they cannot hold out, then we shall likely not fare any better," lamented Craven as he had so few fighters by his side.

As they neared what he estimated was the halfway point between the column and the stricken light cavalrymen, Craven drew them to a standstill just briefly and listened out. The muffled sound of musket and pistol fire could be heard in the distance.

"They fight on!" Jenkins roared.

It also meant they were within galloping distance as musket fire could typically be heard from two miles away.

"Let's move!"

Craven dug in his heels and launched his horse into a rapid

advance as they raced to rescue the cavalrymen before it was too late. He had no idea what they were really getting themselves into, but he was not going to leave his fellow soldiers to die at the hands of the French, not if he had some chance of preventing it. The crack of musket and pistol shots was rapidly growing louder, and a great many shots fired sporadically. Though he had no idea if that was because a great battle was underway or because the French had absolute fire superiority and were raining down volleys on the stricken troops.

Soon they could smell the gunpowder, and the shots were so loud they knew the scene would be in sight in any moment. They came up over a ridge line to find dozens of French cavalrymen dismounted and firing across a deep stream, using trees for cover. About twenty British cavalrymen were on the far side, soaking wet and covered in mud where they had forded the water. There was no sign of their horses. They must have kept their powder dry as they were keeping up a steady stream of fire with pistols and carbines. A dozen or more mounted Frenchmen had clearly travelled far and wide to cross the stream and were now attacking across dry land on their far side. The British soldiers had dragged several fallen trees into place as barricades, and two fought with swords as the French cavalry tried to break through the natural defences of thick foliage and trees all around.

Craven stopped for a brief moment to assess the scene, but Moxy, Ferreira, and Paget already had their rifles in hand and fired. All hitting their targets. Yet many of the Frenchmen now rushed to retrieve their horses from their colleagues who waited at their rear, each man holding the reins of four of their mounts.

"Don't let 'em get in the saddle!" Craven pushed his hand through the sword knot hanging from the guard of his hilt and gave it a few twists to secure it to his wrist before drawing out the blade, "Charge!"

They raced forward, their horses still having enough energy to propel them into a gallop as a cheer rang out from the stricken British cavalrymen who had thought they were fighting to the last man in a deadly last stand. A few of the Frenchmen managed to get into their saddles but others knew they had no time and drew their swords to fight on foot, hoping to use the trees as cover. For scattered skirmishers had no chance against cavalry in open ground.

Craven reached the first Frenchman and cut down with his sword as if to beat through the man's guard as he lifted his sword, but even with the weight of the charge he could not drive through the weapon. The cavalryman's sabre was far heavier than his infantry sword, and his horse was travelling too quickly for a second back handed stroke as he rode on by, and so he left the man to the others as he went on. He reached one Frenchman just as he got into the saddle and ran him through before he could even get his sword from the scabbard.

Cheers continued from the British cavalrymen who went on loading and firing against their attackers on the far side, who were now shaken by the arrival of Craven and his relief party. He saw another Frenchman ready his musket and bring it to the shoulder to shoot at him from just five yards away. Craven let go of his sword, letting it dangle from his wrist by the sword knot and ripped his double-barrelled pistol from its saddle holster. He shot the man dead before turning it on anther who galloped towards him with sabre raised overhead. The ball pierced the man's chest and yet did not stop him from making his cut. Craven let go of his pistol and scooped up his sword back into hand just in time to parry the blow, which shocked his arm and almost beat through his guard. The man crashed the sabre down with all the life he had left in his body before falling from the saddle as his horse rode on.

Vicenta, Charlie, and Birback pursued the enemy relentlessly as if to not let one of them escape with their lives, but Ferreira was already roaring to call them back.

Wheeling back around, Craven could see the French cavalry were being cut to ribbons, with those on the fringe doing their best to escape. Across the water the French cavalry fled the scene also, but still suffered under the fire of the British cavalry who continued firing at their backs, making them pay for what they had done. Craven noticed Hawkshaw in a desperate clash with a French Sergeant. Both men were in the saddle and cut back and forth, yet Hawkshaw didn't fight with his usual fire and skill, and barely made any significant attack at all. The Sergeant raised up in his stirrups to swing a strike, but one foot slipped from the stirrup. He fell forward, exposing his neck to Hawkshaw who had all the time in the world to take the opportunity to end him. Yet he brought his sword up for the cut only to freeze in place, unwilling to bring his blade down against his adversary. The Sergeant finally recovered himself but had lost his sabre as he fell forward, desperately clinging onto the horse. He looked stunned at the glistening blade which was held over his head. He nodded in gratitude for not being slain before riding off as quickly as he could to save his skin.

Shots still rang out and cold steel clashed, but the battle was won as they mopped up the last of the enemy as their friends fled, utterly broken. Many had left their weapons behind in a desperate attempt to flee. Craven rode up to his brother who was still frozen in place, his sword high as if he was stuck there.

"It is done," insisted Craven.

Hawkshaw relaxed a little as he lowered the blade and looked out at the bloodshed all around them.

"I can't do this anymore, not any of it."

Craven felt for him as he had always been a gentle soul. Even in his attempts to do him harm when they first met, he was ever the gentleman.

"I have to get out of here, James, I can't do this anymore," his voice shaky.

But Craven was not having it.

"You can't leave. I won't let you. I need you here."

Hawkshaw looked distraught as he sheathed his sword as if never wanting to draw it again.

"Things will get better. They are already improving now that we are moving forward one again. This must be done, and we must do it. I depend on you. We all do."

Hawkshaw took a deep breath as he looked to the bodies of the dead and wounded, and then to the faces of the friends and comrades he had made and shared so much history with.

"Come on, we are in this together, until the end," pleaded Craven. He reached across and laid a friendly hand on his brother's shoulder.

Hawkshaw said nothing, but finally he nodded in agreement, but he looked no happier about the situation.

"Good show, Sir!" cried out a British cavalry officer as he led the survivors of his troop back across the stream. Two of them needed the support of their fellow soldiers as they could not stand, and several more were walking wounded.

"I should have your name, Sir!" insisted the cavalry officer.

"Major James Craven."

"I will not forget it! I am afraid I am not familiar with your regiment."

"Salford Rifles."

"Riflemen? You fight like hussars!" he yelled as his men clapped and cheered to celebrate their saviours. They soon rounded up enough of the enemy's horses to replace their own as they got back into the saddle once more.

"You are the James Craven who bested General Le Marchant with the sword, are you not?" asked the officer.

"Only on foot. In the saddle the General is a devil."

"Then perhaps you have taken some lessons from him. For you went at the French like devils!"

CHAPTER 8

On the seventh day of the march much of the army made camp at the beautiful town of Castelo de Vide, which sprawled across rolling hills and looked entirely unaffected by the war, and yet a great medieval castle dominated the skyline from which the municipality drew its name. A forty-foot great square tower reached high into the sky atop a well elevated position, providing great commanding views and control for miles all around. The castle had not suffered greatly from the war, and yet they knew it must have been taken by the French in their advance through Portugal, and so must have been taken without much of a fight. It was understandable, considering the retreat to Lisbon by armies and civilians alike. Castelo de Vide was situated halfway up the country of Portugal and on the border with Spain, which explained the significant fortification. However, the mountainous terrain did not allow easy travel between the two nations, especially for an army of significant size. They would have to press on South to the crossing point between the fortresses of Elvas and Badajoz.

"Magnificent, isn't it?" Spring rode up beside them.

Craven and his closest friends imagined they were in a dream. It was not the great castle they looked upon this awe, but the fruitful paradise all around it. It was bordered by the most delightful hills and valleys which produced in abundance the finest fruits such as grapes, pomegranates, oranges, and lemons. It made the paradise smell as good as it looked, and the wine was in such abundance that soldiers at the side of the road boiled meat in it, giving off the most indulgent and mouth-watering odours. After a harsh winter and the brutal conditions, it was a delight for them all that they had to wonder if their eyes betrayed them. It seemed too good to be true.

"Enjoy what little time we have here, Craven, but not too much, you understand?"

Craven nodded in agreement, but Spring wasn't sure if he was really listening as he was lost in the beautiful sights and smells of this stunning heaven.

"I have arranged lodgings for you and your men. This man will take you to them. We may enjoy a few days here."

Spring left them with a local resident to guide them. They were led to a line of homes on the edge of town with ideal grazing land for their horses. The town felt remarkably homely, and the residents welcomed them with open arms, handing out wine upon their arrival. It truly was as if they had arrived in paradise. Food followed the wine, and they made themselves comfortable. It was not long before volunteers came looking for more lessons with sword and bayonet, in spite of all of the food and wine on officer. Craven was both surprised and impressed that they would give up so much to be taught by him. There were now three times as many men seeking lessons than he had been ordered to instruct, but he was not one to turn men away who were so enthusiastic to learn the skills he had spent his lifetime mastering, and like them, he still had so much to learn.

"All this beauty and food and wine, and still you come?" Craven asked with a smile.

"We would all like to live through Badajoz so that we might one day return to the delights of this place," replied one of the officers who had assembled.

"Is it true, Sir, that you do not just teach men to kill the enemy, but to defend their own lives?" asked another.

Craven was taken aback, as he had rarely considered the distinction. The army had taught them to shoot and to kill the enemy, but not the basics of defence and survival in a way which valued their own lives.

"I can't teach you to dodge a cannon ball, but if you can make it to the walls of Badajoz and find yourself locked in combat with sword or bayonet, then I can promise you that you will double your chances of success and survival with a few simple lessons," Craven assured them.

That was all they wanted to hear as they submitted themselves to his exercises. Soon enough they were underway as the clash of singlestick and stave rang out once more. They had been practicing for an hour when several officers on horseback rode up to watch them.

"Sir," said Paget out of concern.

One of the men was Major Rooke, and his two companions looked down upon Craven with as much disgust as the Major did.

"You are Craven?" demanded one of the officers.

"I am, Major James Craven, and you are?"

"Colonel Blakeney," he declared arrogantly as if to lord it over Craven. He paused for a moment as he looked out across the dozens of troops practicing with sticks in hand to resemble musket and bayonet.

"You teach the sword?" he sneered. He had grey mutton chops and must have been in the service for decades, carrying himself like a Lord and expected to be treated as such.

"I do."

"The sword is the weapon of the cavalry, and with which an officer defends his life. What business do these men have with it?" he asked snobbishly.

"I cannot teach these men how to shoot, but they are already quite capable of that. But in this war here in Spain, a man may likely find himself in a battle of cold steel, and I would give that man every chance of victory, for his sake and the army's."

Blakeney laughed.

"You think you know what this army needs, Sir?" he demanded angrily.

"I know what a man must know to defend his life."

"Forgive me, but I find it difficult to believe a man who steals and loots."

"What are you implying?"

"You know very well, Sir, for Major Rooke has informed me of your activities!"

Craven looked furious, but he looked back to Paget and Hawkshaw and knew he owed it to them to keep his temper in check. He could not risk anymore duels.

"Major Rooke is mistaken, Sir, and that much was proven

before the eyes of Lord Wellington himself."

Blakeney grumbled angrily as he dared not speak out against Wellington as much as he evidently wanted to. A lot was expected of Wellington, and he had not yet lived up to those expectations, and many of the officers of the army loathed him for it, even some of the most senior amongst them.

"What do you want from me?" Craven demanded of the Colonel.

"For you to go home and leave the instruction and command of this army to better men, and I shall have it, as God is my witness."

Matthys looked furious as he cursed under his breath. He dared not speak out against an officer but despised the Colonel for using the Lord's name as he condemned Craven, without evidence or reason.

"We cannot let him speak to Craven like that," insisted Paget quietly as he was standing beside the Sergeant.

"That is not for us to decide," whispered Matthys as Blakeney went on.

"If you have such a love of the weapons of our fine troops, then I would have you ensure the quality of them for service. I will send you thirty men every day, and you will instruct them on the correct cleaning procedures of musket and bayonet, and I expect every piece to be in a perfect state."

"Sir, Lord Wellington has instructed me to teach these men how to fight."

"Twelve men each day after the army stops its progression, but we are no longer marching, Major, are we?"

"We are not."

"Then you have more than enough time available to you.

You claim to have the best interests of the men at heart, and I am asking you to ensure their weapons are in the best of condition with which to do so, or do you think me unreasonable?"

Craven shook his head. He was furious, but he dared not cause a scene.

"Make those arms spotless, Major!"

He smirked as though enjoying every second of punishing Craven before turning and leisurely riding away.

"Making friends again, are we?" Ferreira joked.

"That is way out of order, Sir," insisted Paget as he rushed to their side.

"No, that man knows how to drive a dagger deep enough to hurt a man but not kill him," replied Craven.

"What do you mean, Sir?"

"That Colonel does not cause enough offence to protest against, but enough to be an offense anyway," added Matthys.

Moments later a body of men marched in to report to Craven.

"This is Rooke's doing," declared Matthys.

"It is. If he cannot have me kicked out of the army by official means, he means to bully me out."

"How can he do that, Sir?" Paget asked.

"By making my life hell, so that I will quit or make some great mistake, an offense so grievance that Wellington cannot ignore it."

"Then do not, Sir."

"I shall endeavour not to, but that man tries my patience, and there is only so much any man can take."

"I'll do it," insisted Ferreira.

"Do what?"

"See to the cleaning of these weapons. I will have my boys make certain they do not leave with a spot of rust nor a loose flint. Continue your work here, and we will do this."

"I am not sure that is what the Colonel had in mind."

"That bastard expects you to observe the chain of command, and you are quite within your rights to delegate this task to another, for that is what an officer does, do they not? Or does he expect you to clean every musket and bayonet with your own two hands?"

"If he could I am sure he would. Thank you."

"Black powder is my business, and I am damned good at it. Let me do this."

An hour later Colonel Blakeney returned to see double the number of men practicing with sword and bayonet as he had sent to clean their weapons.

"Major Craven!"

"Carry on." Craven went to the Colonel's side.

"Yes, Sir?"

"I gave you an order, Craven, and still you continue on playing these stupid little games."

"Begging your pardon, Sir, but I am conducting Lord Wellington's orders, whilst also facilitating yours," he replied cheekily.

"Is this how you soldier, Craven? Playing games and shirking your responsibilities?"

"I'll tell you how I soldier, Sir. I kill the enemy, and I teach others do it better than they ever could have. But most of all, I give them the tools with which they are best prepared to make it through this war with their bodies in one piece."

"You are a relic, Major," seethed Blakeney, "War is no longer decided by the barbarity of commoners swinging at each other with sticks and swords."

Rooke chuckled quietly to himself, revelling in every moment of Craven's humiliation and discomfort.

"Well, what do you have to say for yourself?" demanded Blakeney as he once again handed Craven a rope with which to hang himself.

"I have fought many battles in this war, Colonel, and every man who serves under me will stand by my teaching. For it has saved their lives and pathed the way to victory."

"You have not won battles. How arrogant of you, Sir. When great regiments of infantry and cavalry have marched this army to victory, and you take credit for their bravery and hard work?"

"Only that which we were responsible," replied Craven calmly.

Blakeney looked furious, for he could not get the rise out of Craven he had hoped for. He was almost boiling over with rage, but he could find no more words as the sound of trotting horses drew their attention. Craven was joyed to see General Le Marchant approaching with a friendly smile on his face. As the cavalry commander drew up before them, Blakeney tried to slip away from the scene.

"Major Craven, still hard at work I see!" Le Marchant roared.

"Indeed, I was just discussing the necessity or lack of the practice of the sword and bayonet here with Colonel Blakeney," replied Craven with a smile.

"Oh, what of it? Do tell, for I am always keen to hear my

fellow officers' thoughts on the matter."

Blakeney was forced to remain but looked sheepish.

"The Colonel believes the need for the practice of sword and bayonet on foot is no longer required, and that we waste our time on such endeavours."

"Is that right?" Le Marchant asked him in amazement.

"Sir, I do believe there are better uses of an infantryman's time, Sir," he declared, trying to put a favourable spin on it.

"Have you ever faced a Frenchman in battle and crossed blades with him?"

"I have not, Sir."

"Then perhaps you might defer to a man who has, for I should hope we would all attempt to learn from the best examples of men of our time?"

"Certainly, Sir, but I am sure we might find fencing masters in England who can assist in these matters."

"We have a master before us here in Major Craven, isn't that right?"

But Craven shrugged in a bumbling fashion as Le Marchant caught sight of Ferreira overseeing the cleaning of musket and bayonet.

"And those men there, they are not Salfords?"

Blakeney opened his mouth to speak but could not get a word in, as Craven jumped at his opportunity.

"No, Sir, Colonel Blakeney requested that we oversee the cleaning of the arms of the infantry."

Le Marchant paused for a moment, looking to Blakeney with disgust as he finally realised what was happening there. This was not a friendly argument over the best qualities of a soldier and his training. It was an attempt to bully Craven.

"I...I," began Blakeney as he tried to find a way to justify himself.

"For shame, Colonel. You will put an end to this immediately."

"I only..." he began again.

"I will not hear it. You will not pile your needless duties on this man to fuel your own prejudices, Sir."

"I did not..."

"No, Colonel, you will not interrupt me! This work detail will end immediately, and you will not interfere with Major Craven or any of those under his command or supervision. Do I make myself clear?"

"Yes, Sir," replied Blakeney with gritted teeth.

He hated every moment of it but was utterly powerless to act.

"Well? Be on your way, Sir."

Blakeney turned to leave with his tail between his legs, and Rooke looked even more disappointed.

"Thank you," said Craven.

"I expect discipline. I demand it in fact, but I will not tolerate a bully and an oppressor."

Ferreira had listened in to every word and was already sending the infantrymen on their way before waiting to finish up the job he had taken on board to lift the weight from Craven's soldiers. Craven breathed a sigh of relief that it was finally over, but a cry rang out which attracted all their attention, including Blakeney and Rooke. Quicks came running into view with a look of panic on his face and carrying a string of sausages in one hand as he fled with a local woman chasing him with a broom in hand.

"Stop there!" Le Marchant roared.

Quicks came to a halt before them, but the woman smacked him with the broom anyway before Ferreira rushed in to restrain her.

"What is the meaning of this?" demanded Le Marchant as Blakeney and Rooke watched on with glee, looking for another chance to stick a knife into Craven's back. Ferreira communicated with her briefly.

"She says he stole from her."

"Is this true?" Le Marchant demanded of the former pickpocket who Craven had recruited in England upon their brief return home. He nodded shamefully and with fear and regret in his eyes.

"These people give up their homes and wine and food, and still you steal more from them?" Craven cried out angrily.

"This is a most grievous offence for which Lord Wellington has decried much of late!" Blakeney piped up.

Craven sighed as his shoulders drooped in despair, for he knew the Colonel had got his hands wrapped firmly about their necks once more.

"Quite so, I am afraid," agreed Le Marchant.

"I am sorry, Sir, I just…" apologised Quicks.

"There is no answer you can give to justify stealing from the people we came here to help. These people are our allies!" Le Marchant shouted angrily.

"We must call for the provosts!" Blakeney demanded.

"No!" Craven would not give over one of his own.

"This man has committed a most heinous crime and must be dealt with accordingly," barked Blakeney.

"And he will be, but as his commanding officer, it is my responsibility."

"Well then, Major, what will you do to this ill-disciplined thief?"

Craven was deeply conflicted as he looked to Le Marchant, who felt for him, too, but he knew he must take severe action, or worse would be done to Quicks by others. All eyes were on Craven as they waited to see what punishment he would deliver. Ferreira took the sausages from him and gave them back to the woman he had stolen them from.

"Give my sincerest apologies and assure her that this man will be punished for his crimes," he said to Ferreira.

The woman did not look happy about it as she snatched away the sausages and sighed, leaving without another word to them but mumbling angrily to herself. Blakeney and Rooke were near salivating as they watched the scene unfold, relishing the anguish Craven was experiencing. They imagined he would let his man go free if it were not for the witnesses who now watched with anticipation for the punishment which must surely follow.

"It was just a few sausages, Sir," insisted Quicks.

Craven looked to Le Marchant for some way out of what was expected of him, but there was none. Quicks had sealed his own fate.

"It's not just a few sausages. You stole food from our allies, from the people of this land who we expect to treat us as if we're their own countrymen."

Quicks sighed as his head sank, knowing a severe punishment would follow and there was no fighting it now.

"Lord Wellington has made it quite clear that those who steal from the local populace must face severe punishment and discipline. A flogging. One hundred lashes," declared Craven.

"One hundred!" Blakeney roared incredulously, "It should

be two hundred!"

"He is the Major's man, and the number is at his discretion," snapped Le Marchant.

Blakeney was silenced but still smiled at what he deemed a success. He watched the Salford Rifles formed up so that the punishment might be conducted with the proper military conduct, and not how Paget had done when he had lost his temper.

Three wooden staves were tied into a tripod as the Salford Rifles did not use the Sergeant's spontoon which was normally used for such an affair. Quicks was shaking as he took off his shirt and had his hands bound to the tripod. A Drum Major from another regiment stepped up with the whip to do the task. Few men enjoyed it, but they could be admonished for striking with too little vigour and letting off their victim too easily, so much so that men sometimes died from the horrible beatings they received under such corporal punishment.

"One hundred lashes, begin!"

A slow drumbeat tapped out the lash in slow time as the Drum Major went to work. It was an awful sight for all who knew him, but not for Blakeney and Rooke who saw it as a great triumph over the man they had set their sights on. Le Marchant had stayed by Craven's side to ensure the two hateful officers did not cause any more trouble, but he was as disgusted by the sight as Quicks' friends and comrades.

"A terrible thing," he whispered to Craven.

"Yes, and he needed to be punished, but not like this."

Quicks groaned in pain as the first twenty-five lashes came to an end, and the Drum Major passed the duties on to one of the drummers to continue the punishment so that it might be shared by several men. Also, so that they were fresh to strike hard enough as to do serious harm. Craven glared at Blakeney and Rooke with murderous intent but said and did nothing as they looked back with a similar level of disrespect. The second set of twenty-five lashes were completed, and Quicks dropped a little, only suspended by the bindings at his wrists as he was too weak to stand. The drummer handed over the cat o'nine tails to the next man as only half the job was done, and he got into position to continue.

"He's had enough!"

Craven drew the punishment to a close after half of what he had condemned the man to. The drummer stopped immediately, glad to not have to carry out the grisly duty.

"Enough?" Blakeney cried.

"This is the Major's responsibility, and we can all see that justice has been served. That man will live with the marks of this for the rest of his life and suffer the shame and pain for many weeks and months to come," declared Le Marchant as he brought an end to any debate over the matter.

Craven rushed to Quicks' side to help untie him as a surgeon approached and two men with a stretcher in case he needed it.

"A fine display of discipline, if only it had lasted longer," declared Blakeney sadistically as he and Rooke rode on.

"A sad affair, but I too must be on my way, and I am sorry it is not under better circumstances," said Le Marchant as Quicks dropped into Craven's hands. He was barely conscious and delirious.

"Thank you, for everything," said Craven, knowing Le Marchant had gone far out of his way to help.

"Good luck, Craven, and may you not cross paths with those pathetic excuses for men again."

"I wish it were so, but I fear it is not."

Le Marchant nodded in appreciation as he left them, and Matthys help place Quicks down face first on the stretcher. His back was badly lacerated and covered in blood as though he had run a gauntlet of sabres. Hawkshaw paced up to get a closer look when he turned pale and vomited. Paget rushed to help him, but Hawkshaw got himself upright and pushed the Lieutenant away. His eyes were wide as if he were about to break down.

"No more, no more, not anymore!"

He dropped to his knees and began to sob as the weight of all they had seen and done was finally too much pressure on his shoulders. Nobody knew how to react as he was a brave and fearsome fighter who they had all witnessed run and ride into hellfire beside them.

"Get him inside!" Craven would not see his brother suffer further humiliation before the troops, even though none had a bad word to say about him. For many shared a little of his melancholic state.

"I've got him. Go to your brother," declared the surgeon as he knew they all had a lot on their plate.

Paget and Ferreira helped the sobbing Captain into a nearby house where they had been billeted. Everyone looked to Craven for answers as it was indeed a bleak day.

"Get back to your training!"

He then rushed on after his brother, but he reached the door to the house to see Hawkshaw was in no better a state. He was slumped down and looked entirely exhausted, not just by the day but by life. He was broken, for the sight of one of them own mutilated by their very hands had pushed a troubled mind over the edge. Craven could not enter the room as he watched from outside. Ferreira and Paget tried to console his brother. He heard movement and jumped a little. He was on edge now, too, but relaxed as he realised it was Matthys who had come to give aid to him, despite Hawkshaw being the man most in need.

"What can we do for him?" Craven whispered.

"We can do as he asked us to. We can let him go."

Craven shook his head in despair as he despised the idea.

"Remember who we are, James. Every man is here because he chooses to be, and not because he is pressed into service. That is what we are and that is a strength. You cannot drag him along this road any further. Let him go, and perhaps one day he will come back to us, but if you press him to stay by your side, I fear there will be many more tears and far worse scenes."

Craven looked to his sobbing brother and felt a deep sadness overcome him, not only for seeing the state of Hawkshaw, but because he knew Matthys was right. He nodded in agreement as he finally accepted what must be done.

CHAPTER 9

Soon enough they were on the road once more, making their way to Badajoz. Every soldier in the army knew where they were going and what was expected of them, and everything would be at stake. For whoever stormed the fortress would be in for death or glory, or perhaps both, yet there was also anticipation and excitement amongst the troops as they were eager to be pressing forward once more. They marched on through a dreary and drizzly day, and Craven often stopped to look back at Quicks. He marched with them despite recovering from the flogging, perhaps because it was better than riding in the bumpy and rickety bone shaking carts acquired from the locals which were so often used for carrying casualties. The young pickpocket looked most distraught, and Craven so desperately wanted to go and speak with him, but there was no time, not until they stopped for the night.

"He will be okay," insisted Matthys as he coughed. He'd

seen Craven looking back at the man he had been forced to put to the lash.

"How can you be so sure?"

"He isn't the first man to be flogged, nor the first of us to go through some hardship. He is sore now, but in time he will recognise his wrongdoing."

"You think I was right to do it, then?"

"Punishment was required. Flogging is rarely the right path in my eyes, and you well know, but you had no choice. You were between a rock and a hard place with that Colonel Blakeney."

"Yes, and I do not think it is the last we will see of him."

"Success puts a target on your back, you know that. It's always been like that. You remember the old days," replied Matthys as he thought of their gladiatorial past.

Back then they only played at war. The gladiatorial fights of the day were nothing like the deadly displays of the Roman eras, which could leave the ground awash with blood to appease a rabid mob. Craven smiled as he thought back to those days.

"It was a far simpler time," he mused.

"Would you go back to it if you could? Instead of all this?"

Craven thought about it for a few moments before looking back at the column of friends he had made along the way.

"Not for the world," he smiled.

"I could never have imagined that your path could have been this. A hero in Wellington's army. A far cry from cudgelling at villages across England and drunken fights in the gutter."

Craven smiled in agreement as it felt like a lifetime ago, both in time and the sort of life they now led.

"Quicks, why would he do it?" Craven could not stop thinking about the awful situation he had found himself in, "I never thought I would have to flog one of our own."

"You have done worse, but not gotten caught."

Craven shrugged, unable to deny he had not taken a great deal that was not his throughout his lifetime.

"This is different. I have taken from other soldiers, from our officers, from the enemy, but Quicks, he took from the people we came here to fight for."

"A few years ago, you would not have seen them any differently. You would have taken from them just as he did. You've changed, and remember that, for Quicks can change, too. You gave him an opportunity here, but none of us can change all that we are in a few days or weeks. Do not give up on him."

"Flogging can do a lot of things to a man, and most of them are unfavourable at best."

"He will take his licks and keep going forward, the same as the rest of us."

Craven groaned in agreement. He hoped Matthys was right, but he was far from certain about the outcome.

"We will make camp away from the army tonight. I would not have another encounter with that bastard Blakeney. I don't care if we have to sleep under the night's sky."

The flogging had brought an ill mood to them all that was hard to shake, but as the day came to a close, the army found quarters amongst a town and the small hamlets for several miles around. Craven led them into a quiet little valley where the locals greeted them like returning heroes. They offered up food and shelter for the night, which lifted the mood of them all significantly. A great fire was lit so that everyone could gather together that evening. The homes and barns were too cramped for so many people and only one house possessed a fireplace. Craven had been given the privilege of billeting there that night, along with several of his closest officers and friends. He watched from the doorway of the house with a cup of wine in hand as the troops and locals mingled. A hundred light infantrymen had also made the tranquil valley their home for the night and joined in the festivities, as if it were a great holiday. The soldiers significantly outnumbered the local populace, which was little over fifty people. He watched Ferreira retell the events of the war to a great many of the locals. He spoke very quickly in his own language, for these were his countrymen and they conversed at such a speed Craven could not understand a word, despite having gained a grasp of a little Portuguese in his time. But he smiled as the crowd excitedly clung onto the Portuguese Captain's every word.

"It is a good feeling, Sir, is it not?" Paget asked.

Craven nodded in agreement.

"This is what we came here to do, to drive the French out of these lands, and we are finally doing it. Soon enough we will step into Spain again just as we did at Rodrigo, and the gates to the country will open before us."

"The Spanish people have been under French rule far longer than these people. Imagine how they will welcome us!" Paget roared excitedly.

"So long as we can keep moving forward this time."

It weighed on all their minds. The last time they made an advance across Spain was to fight at Talavera when Paget was still fresh faced and getting to know Craven. Almost three years had passed since that incredible affair, and yet they still had not made any progress in Spain since having been driven back into Portugal.

"We will do it this time, won't we, Sir?"

"We can keep doing this, outmanoeuvring the enemy, attacking where they do not expect, and in the winter when they least expect it. But eventually, one day, we will have to fight the French army. Not the garrisons of town and cities. Not a small force, but an army."

"Have you not done so before?"

"We have fought on the back foot as we fled to Lisbon, and we have chased a hungry and exhausted force out of the country, but somewhere out there is the real army. The army that chased us all the way to Corunna. One day we will have to face them in open battle at a place of their choosing, and then this war will be decided."

"In one battle?" Paget was horrified.

"That is the one that will matter, for us anyway. For if the French lose a great battle, they will merely send another army to oppose us, but when that time comes, when all that Wellington has faces the main French army in Spain, we cannot lose. For there is no other army to replace this one."

"When, Sir? When will this happen?"

"Soon, it has to. We are pressing into Spain. They will find us, and there will be nothing more for it. There will be no running or hiding. We must face them head on and smash them into the ground."

"And if we do not?"

"Then we go back to England and prepare to defend our own borders."

"All of this will hinge on one single battle?"

"It will, and Wellington knows it, and so he will not go into such a battle lightly or without a great deal of preparation."

"What can we do, Sir? What can we do to give us the greatest chance of success?"

"Only what we are already doing. Weaken the enemy wherever we can, so that when that battle comes, they are stretched thin and lacking in confidence."

"Confidence, Sir?"

"Yes, just as in a fight with cold steel between two men. We do not want to fight a French army who has absolute belief in their own strength and capability. We want them to be on edge, to feel that they are vulnerable. We want them to run when they face us."

"And will they?"

Craven sighed as he knew it was a lot to ask.

"You've seen how bloody a fight can be when neither side will back down and flee like they should. When the battle comes, Wellington cannot afford a fight like that. None of us can," admitted Craven as he thought about his brother's breakdown and how others could easily follow in the face of such extreme bloodshed which lay ahead.

"Look, Sir." Paget drew his attention to a glimmer of movement at the edge of the crowd. It was Quicks, carrying all of his equipment, and they both knew that could only mean one thing. He intended to desert.

"Shit!"

Craven thrust his cup of wine into Paget's hands so that he could go on and intervene. He stormed over towards the man he had flogged as he walked off towards the darkness and vanished behind a barn. Craven upped his pace to catch up with him but stopped as he reached the edge of the barn to get a good look for himself and not give away his position. He did not want to cause a fight or for Quicks to vanish into the night.

"Wait." Matthys had quietly joined Craven, having kept a keen eye on all happenings as he always did. Craven looked hesitant to do as Matthys suggested. He desperately wanted to go forward and say some words.

"We can't let him go," whispered Craven as they were within earshot.

"No but look." Matthys pointed out to where another figure stepped up towards Quicks. It was Corporal Nooth, the man who had most protested Quicks joining them. A prideful man who had nearly defeated Craven upon the scaffold with singlesticks. He had proudly worn the uniform of the militia and looked down upon Quicks as nothing more than a petty thief living in the gutter. Craven could not imagine how this situation could end well, but Matthys had faith and held him back as they watched and listened.

"You are leaving us?" Nooth asked him calmly.

"I will desert if I have to," replied Quicks.

"Because of the flogging?"

"Why would I stay? Who would stay for that?"

"I see how it is."

"What do you mean by that?" Quicks answered angrily.

"You are blaming everyone else for what was done to you. I suppose you blame Craven, and Blakeney, and Wellington himself, don't you?"

"I didn't flog myself," he spat back.

"Yes, yes you did. You got yourself into this trouble, and

you are also the only one who can get you out of it. Craven took a big chance on you. You were nothing before you put on that uniform. A common thief living off of scraps with no family, no meaning or purpose, just others like you. You lived like a sewer rat."

"Not by choice. I was not lucky enough to be born into a good family with a trade and a home and all of the things you could want for."

"No, you had a shit start and shit luck, and nobody will deny that. But here, Craven gave you the chance to leave all that behind and climb as high as you were willing to push yourself. You could not have asked for a greater opportunity, and few men ever get it, and I think you know it. You slipped back into your old ways, and you made a mistake, but that does not need to destroy your hopes for the future."

"Why do you even care?"

"I used to hate you, and maybe for those first few weeks I would have stood aside and watched you run with glee. Perhaps I even would have given you a push in that direction, but I was wrong. The moment we put on these tunics we became brothers, and nothing can ever change that, except you and me. One of us can forsake the other, but no other force in this world can come between us, not even death. You are my brother, and I will fight for you, even if it is your own foolishness that I must do battle with."

Quicks sighed as he looked out into the distance, now deeply conflicted whilst before being fully confident in his decision to flee.

"You think of me as a brother?" he finally asked.

"I know it, and whilst we remain true to one another we

always will be."

"I don't want to go. I don't even know where I would go," he admitted.

"Then don't. You have made one mistake, but you have received your punishment and it is done now. It is in the past. Do no ruin this for what is in the past."

Quicks began to tear up as the two embraced as brothers, and Quicks relaxed. It was over. He was not going anywhere now.

Craven breathed a sigh of relief as he knew the young man would almost certainly get himself killed if he went through his planned desertion, whether it be by the enemy, hanged by the provosts, ripped apart by wolves, or murdered by guerrillas.

"You see, you must believe in those around you. For there are many capable soldiers under your command," declared Matthys as they moved out of sight.

"That was quite something," admitted Craven as he was proud of them both.

"Is everything okay, Sir?" Paget approached with Craven's wine cup in hand, which he took back gladly.

"It is indeed," he smiled and led them back to the fire where great conversation ensued. Ferreira still regaled the locals of all of the things they had seen and done and the news as he understood it. Soon enough Nooth and Quicks came to join them, his equipment and weapon no longer in hand.

"A good night?" Craven asked them.

"Yes, it is, Sir," admitted Quicks. He had been terrified for what the future held as he went out into the world all alone, as he had been for most of his life. A great weight had been lifted from his shoulders, and he carried himself a little taller now that he had Nooth in his corner.

Craven and Paget soon returned to the house that would be their home for the night. The roaring fire inside was a luxury they rarely knew, for the few houses with fireplaces were always occupied by the most senior officers, and yet in this valley, Craven was that officer.

"You knew he was going to desert, didn't you, Sir?" Paget finally asked, having figured it out for himself.

"Yes," admitted Craven.

"Would you have let him?"

"Yes. If he had chosen to go through with it, I would have had no choice but to seal his fate, or I could let him go and hope the best for him."

"I never understood desertion. It always seemed a coward's path, but I see now I was wrong to think that. Seeing the way Captain Hawkshaw was struck down by the horrors we have all seen. That could have been any one of us, and we do not know how much a man can take until the last of his strength fails. For many officers they may choose to go home or take up some office far from the war, but for the enlisted men, they have no such choice. We work them until their breaking point, and then we punish them because they were driven to do awful things," pondered Paget.

"That is why John Moore was right." Craven was referring to the officer who had been instrumental in the development of the light infantry and had led the retreat to Corunna.

"Really, Sir? I never had the privilege of meeting the General."

"He was before your time," smiled Craven.

"What sort of man was he, Sir?"

"One that believed in making every soldier the best that he could be, not with the lash, but by rewarding men for their achievements and encouraging them on to great heights. The likes of which they scarcely believed possible."

"Is that why you do not flog men, Sir?"

"That, and I would want to murder any man who tried to flog me."

"I can understand that, Sir. For even the thought of it revolts me. Do you believe Quicks can rise from this and become the soldier he once was?"

"A man can come back from the very worst hell, and I know, because I have, and I have seen others do so in far worse a place."

That sentiment calmed Paget significantly as it brought a great warmth to his heart. It reminded him why he had such a great love for the Salford Rifles and those who he served beside.

The great warmth of the fire soon made them drowsy, and they both fell into a deep sleep, but they were awoken in the early hours of the next morning by the shrill scream of a woman. Craven's eyes shot open. The sound was muffled and a little distance away, but they heard it again. He shot to fit feet as Paget joined him. Both men rushed outside with their sword belts in hand, looking for the source of distress. The adrenaline had caused them both to be wide awake in a split second. They turned a bend to see Ferreira hauling one of the light infantry soldiers out of a small shed with his trousers hanging about his ankles and holding his long shirt covering his private parts. Ferreira looked furious as he grabbed hold of the staggering man and gave him a hard back handed slap.

"What is the meaning of this?" Craven demanded.

A crowd was already gathering of both the Salford Rifles and the light infantryman's companions. Craven rushed to the scene to find a woman cowering in the shed and trying to cover herself up with her ripped dress. He looked to Ferreira for answers, though he already knew what he was looking upon.

"The wretch had his way with that woman," Ferreira growled angrily as he held on to the Englishman who he believed had raped one of his countrymen. Paget rushed into the shed, and upon sight of the woman he dropped his sword belt and took off his tunic to put over her.

"What happened here?"

"Ask her," demanded Craven of Ferreira.

The two exchanged a few words, but the woman would not even make eye contact as she mumbled in return.

"This man forced himself upon her," replied Ferreira for all to hear.

"I did not. She opened her legs for me!" spat the man with a bloody mouth.

Craven felt a rage boil over inside of him as he thought back to the punishment dealt out to Quicks for the offence of stealing food, the lashes he had been dealt as a result. He despised having to punish soldiers, but for an offence this severe he did not have any doubts.

"Come on, Sir, she wanted it," insisted the man.

But Craven was not having it, and neither was Paget who reached for his sword, gripping the sheathed weapon strongly as if wanted to deal out justice with his own hand.

"Captain, a firing squad if you will," Craven ordered Ferreira.

Some of the man's companions began to protest, but

Charlie ripped her sabre from her side and waved it before them. Caffy stepped up to support her, not needing anything but his own bare hands to intimidate them.

"Sergeant Barros!" Ferreira kept a firm grasp on his prisoner as he led him to the wall of the shed where he had committed his crime, as his victim was walked away by Paget. Ferreira slammed him against the wall before drawing out his sword.

"Move, and I will run you through myself."

He stepped up to the five men Sergeant Barros had assembled to do the duty. They all knew what the man's crime was, and so there was no hesitation for what they must do. Not even Matthys interfered, as tensions were high and he wanted to see justice done, even if he knew they were wrong to do so.

"Make ready!" Craven ordered.

The rifles were brought to full cock.

"Sir, you can't do this!" cried the man.

"Present!"

Few believed they would go through with it, but Craven did not hesitate for even a second.

"Fire!"

The rifles erupted and a cloud of smoke filled the scene. Every single ball found its mark as the soldier was riddled with lead and collapsed down dead before he had even touched the ground. His companions looked appalled but dared not say anything and bring Craven's wrath down upon them. They could see with their own eyes that he was not a man to be trifled with.

"Get him in the ground!" Craven ordered of them. For he would not have his own comrades waste their time with such a chore.

The light infantrymen soon retrieved the body of their man and carried him away to bury him in a field nearby.

"You shouldn't have done that." Matthys stepped up beside Craven who was still shaking with anger.

"Yes, I should, and I did," he seethed.

CHAPTER 10

Timmerman shot awake and fell off his bed at the sound of his door being thunderously thrown open. He got up and reached for a knife to realise it was Craven who had forced his way into his room.

"God, Craven, what cannot wait until I was on my own two feet?" he demanded as he rubbed his sore head from all the wine he had consumed the night before.

"Soult's treasure horde, can it still be done?"

Timmerman took a seat on his bed before thinking about what Craven had said and realising he was back in the game. He smirked greedily, imagining the riches which lay in their future.

"The timing has never been better. If we set off today, we can take it all."

"Then we take it all. One hour and we will be on our way."

Timmerman sprang to his feet as he felt himself relieved at the renewal of his grand and devious scheme.

"What changed your mind?"

"It's time we put our closest friends first for once. Badajoz is coming soon enough, so let us take what we can get whilst we have the chance."

Craven stormed away without any more explanation. Timmerman quickly grabbed for his clothing as he enthusiastically prepared to move out. He burst out of the house to find Paget and Matthys awaiting him, both looked on disapprovingly.

"You don't agree? I don't care," declared Craven.

"Taking from the enemy and diminishing them, no, I do not have any problem with that, but what you did back there, there will come a time when a price must be paid for it," declared Matthys, referring to the firing squad.

"I will stand beside you all the way," insisted Paget.

"Then what is the problem?"

"We have our orders, Sir. We are to instruct the troops in the sword and bayonet."

"We have more than enough capable swordsmen who can conduct those duties. The Salford Rifles will continue to march with the army."

"You are playing a dangerous game," added Matthys.

"Always," smirked Craven as he led them back to their lodgings, walking past the burial party still digging the grave of the man he'd had shot. Two of the men looked upon Craven with disgust, but he paid them no attention.

"You should watch your back, for having men look at you with such fury is a dangerous thing," insisted Matthys.

"Men have looked at me like that my whole life. Let them come and try and take my blood!"

He was still fuming over the rape of the local woman.

"Sir, are you sure we should be leaving the army now?" Paget asked.

"I've had enough of this. It is time we do what we do best."

They reached their own troops who were as eager to move on as he was. He hadn't told many about Timmerman's ambitious caper, and he could not share it with them all. He signalled for his closest friends to come to him, mostly the ones who had been with him since Talavera, but also a few he had found along the way such as Vicenta and Amyn. They gathered around with Ferreira also.

"What is happening here?" asked the Portuguese Captain.

"We're going after Soult's treasure," smiled Craven.

"I thought you'd given up on that?"

"What can I say, I was a fool."

"Okay, and it can be done?"

"Yes."

"Safely?"

"When can anyone assure safety at times like this? We are at war."

"Presently we are billeted with an army and do not have to keep watch at night, waiting for the French to pounce on us."

"And in a few weeks' time we will be storming Badajoz. If we survive that damned place, would you not rather be a rich man to enjoy the life that follows?"

"I didn't join the army to become a rich man."

"Because you didn't know it was an option, but I am telling you that it is. You cannot tell me you have not dreamt of being a wealthy man? Or would you live out your life on the pension of a soldier?"

Ferreira groaned, as it was clearly something he had fretted over. He had become accustomed to a decadent life since knowing Craven, even if it did come at a high cost and risk.

"Well? What do you say?"

Ferreira looked to Matthys for an honest opinion as he knew he would get it.

"Well?"

"It's not the worst idea nor the stupidest thing our fearless leader has asked us to do, and perhaps some good can come of it. I could do a lot to help a great deal of people when I get back to England if I have plenty of coin to do it."

"All right, then, let's do it."

"You won't regret it."

"I don't know about that, but if we end up living the rest of this war as prisoners of war, I will never let you forget it."

"The secret to crime, my dear Captain, is to not get caught," smirked Craven.

The rest of them laughed aloud, and even Matthys saw the funny side, as he saw no evil in stealing from an enemy who stole from everyone to amass his fortune.

"Will we not be missed, Sir?"

"Mr Paget, our orders are to instruct a small body of men each afternoon and evening, and there is no reason that will stop. Wellington gave me the power to operate independently in the field, and that is just what we will do."

"I am not sure he gave it so that we could go after a treasure hoard."

"The most important aspect of our job is to cause chaos amongst the enemy. We attack their supply and communication lines. We counter their scouting efforts. We make life an absolute misery for the French and lead them on a road to ruin. That is what Wellington wanted from us, and this is precisely what we will do. Soult commands one of the largest armies in all of Spain, can you think of a better way to hurt and weaken him than taking his riches?"

Paget shrugged as it was hard to argue with that.

"We are going to win this war, but I'll be damned if I do not come out of it a rich man, all of us rich men," declared Craven.

A cheer rang out as that was the dream for all of them, even Matthys who dreamed of the good he could do with the power of money to back his efforts.

"Gamboa will lead the Salfords onward, but the rest of us, we ride. Let's move!"

They gathered their things and mounted up as they watched the army begin to march on. Twenty-one riders were all they could muster as they departed from the column and made for open ground. It was not long before they were once again in beautiful and tranquil rural lands far from any towns or villages. As they approached a crossroads up ahead, they could see Timmerman waiting for them with fifteen of his own men all mounted and ready for the adventure they had ahead of them. The sight of the Major used to strike fear into the hearts of many of them, but he was a welcoming sight now. They all knew what he had done for Craven. He was still a rogue, but he was their kind of rogue, for he fought with them and not against them.

"Where is your brother?" Timmerman asked, having long buried the hatchet with the man who had slept with his wife, but still eager to rib him in good jest.

"He returns to England."

"Wounded?" Timmerman was genuinely concerned.

"Yes, though not in any way you could see."

"You have broken him," declared Timmerman.

Craven sighed as that was in many ways accurate and true.

"A little time away and the comforts of home can do wonders to heal a man's heart and soul. I do not believe it will be the last we see of the Captain. He was born to the sword and no man with his skills stays away for long."

Craven looked stunned and had to wait for a punchline for a moment, assuming his old adversary was mocking him and his brother, but after a short time passed, he realised Timmerman was genuine, and he was speechless.

"We should be on our way," insisted Paget.

"Yes, we should. I will lead the way." Timmerman turned his horse about and led his small party on. Craven was still speechless as he did not know what to think about the change in Timmerman.

"If this war can change you, it can change anyone," declared Matthys as he provided an answer to Craven's bewilderment.

"You think he has become a good man?"

"I think he has become a better man than he was."

Craven thought on it for a few moments, realising he was no different and that was what Matthys was getting at as he rode on after Timmerman's troop.

"Do you believe this will work?"

"Timmerman is a wild one, but he has survived this long, and there is a lot to be said for that. He takes risks, but always calculated ones. If he thinks this can be done, then I am inclined to believe there is a good chance of success."

Craven sighed.

"The last time we went after a baggage train on his advice didn't go so well."

"Neither have many of your ideas," smiled Matthys.

Paget rode up beside them.

"Sir, if these wagons contain such great riches, will they not be guarded by an entire army?"

"Soult cannot assign such a force without attracting a great deal of attention. And I imagine Napoleon himself would want a sizeable share of all that he has taken to pay for the war efforts, and he cannot spare the men. The siege of Cadiz still goes on."

"Still? It has been two years," replied Paget in amazement as he remembered their role in that affair, and it felt a lifetime ago, just like Talavera.

"A long siege indeed, a thorn in Napoleon's side, an embarrassment even," declared Craven.

"Can they continue to hold out?"

"So long as we continue to threaten them here along the border with Portugal, yes, for they cannot spare the troops to do what is needed to capture the city."

Paget sighed.

"What is it?"

"We forever seem strung out, spread far across the lands, just as the French are. Never strong enough to do what must be done."

"We captured Rodrigo, did we not?"

Paget nodded in agreement.

"And Badajoz will follow."

"You are sure?"

"Certain. Once again, this army moves earlier than the enemy could have expected. Our spies say the enemy expected Wellington to regroup and wait for the spring before moving on Badajoz."

"And so they fell for the same trick twice?"

Craven chuckled.

"Indeed."

"They shall not fall for it a third time," added Paget.

"They won't need to. For by the time we are through with Badajoz the spring will be upon us and the campaigning season will begin once more. Armies will be able to move freely, and the great battle will finally be upon us."

"Where will it be fought, Sir?" Paget asked excitedly as if it were the Battle of Armageddon, the prophesied final battle between men and God. For many soldiers it might as well be Armageddon, for it could well seal the fates of them all.

"Somewhere out there in Spain," mused Craven.

He looked out to the East, the very direction they were now travelling as they made their way deep into mountains and the remote tracks which would lead them into the neighbouring country. The sorts of tracks used by guerrillas, spies, and scouts, but never passable by anything that might be considered an army. It was the great geographical divide between the two nations. There were only two main roads between the two countries, each guarded by the great fortress towns they now fought over. They went on, finding no other signs of people along the way until making camp for the night. They settled down low in a valley where they might have campfires and not be seen far away in the distance. They could not risk alerting the enemy to their presence, nor could they manage without some warmth for the night, as they were still in the last clutches of winter.

Craven took a seat beside a fire where his closest friends had gathered, but to his surprise Timmerman pushed his way in to sit beside him.

"I hear you shot a man by firing squad," he smiled.

Craven shrugged.

"You did? Not even one of your own, I hear?"

"He raped a local woman. He's lucky I gave him a quick death."

Timmerman looked amazed.

"I suppose you'd have let it go. Let the man go on without even a scolding?"

"Why is it you think so little of me, Craven?"

"Because you've given me good reason to."

"That fair, but no. I'll do a lot of things many men would not, but not that, nor would I allow any man to do so. If I caught one of mine doing something like that, I wouldn't be calling up a firing squad. I'd shoot him myself."

Craven nodded in agreement and appreciated the fact that his old enemy had some moral standards. In fact, they were far greater than he would have expected.

"And all of the women I have seen you and your boys with?"

"Whores, or local women who were happy to keep us company."

"More of the former, I imagine," smirked Craven.

"You might be surprised. We are liberators to many of these towns and villages, and many are eager to show their appreciation."

"Birback laughed along in agreement, as he had certainly enjoyed the company of more than a few enthusiastic young women. And several others laughed along before falling silent once more as they watched the crackling fire, mesmerised by the flickering lights and most thankful for the warmth as they held out their hands to the blaze.

"What will you do when this war is over?" Craven asked Timmerman.

"What?" he asked in surprise.

"Men often ask me what I will do when this is over, what I would do. I am not sure I even have the answers because what I was doing before seems to be of little importance anymore. And you? What will you do?"

"Well, I am a gentleman, and so I will go on being a gentleman."

"That is neither a career nor a calling."

"I beg to differ, for the gentlemanly pursuits fill one's time with ease. I will hunt and I will ride. I will shoot and play cards. I will attend great dinners and insult the fair natured folk. A gentleman has much to live up to," declared Timmerman proudly.

"A life of enjoyment and excess? That sounds like my old life, only with rather more money and position. That's not a career. That is the pursuit of your passions."

"Precisely."

Craven laughed.

"What of it?"

"Most men here must occupy their time with work to earn money with which to live," added Paget, who finally had begun to understand the way most people lived.

"Not you?"

"No, but it may be when I return, for I do not go back to my family fortune. I have nothing but this career."

"You can't make your fortune in the Army!" Timmerman laughed.

Craven nodded in agreement, for many officers bankrupted themselves to keep up the lifestyle of an officer. The pay was low and the costs high, especially when trying to keep up with the higher ranks, which one must if he was to seek promotion. The Salford Rifles were very different. The officers did not live apart from the men and spend vast amounts on mess fees.

"It seems you need this treasure more than me," laughed Timmerman.

There was a solemn silence as it was no laughing matter. As for the rest of them, a life of leisure as he described was nothing more than a dream. That left Craven deep in thought about what he wanted for his future and the future of them all. He finally drifted off to sleep. He awoke to find a weary group of friends around him with little enthusiasm for going on, and so he shot up with as much vibrancy as he could.

"Come on, lads, we've got a fortune to claim!"

They were soon on their way, but it would be another day and night before they could reach their target. And none of them were quite sure how they would get such a heavy wealth of money and treasure back into safe lands, considering the mountainous terrain they had crossed. On the third day at noon, they were finally brought to a halt by Moxy who had been riding far out ahead of them with Vicenta by his side. Craven and Timmerman dismounted and approached carefully and quietly so they could look out behind the ridge where they now looked down into the next valley.

"Would you look at that," marvelled Timmerman.

"Is it them?"

"Has to be."

They studied several heavily laden French wagons. One was stuck in the wet mud where it had fallen down at the edge of the road into a ditch. The drivers and soldiers assigned to protect the wagons were attempting to drag it free by pushing and pulling from both sides as they tried to rock it free without success.

"If it wasn't for them getting stuck, we might never have caught them."

"And whose fault is that? You dithered for many days. We are lucky we still had a chance at this," replied Timmerman.

But Craven was busy studying the scene.

"It's a lot of protection for four wagons," he declared. For there were near one hundred soldiers escorting them, "Three to one?" he asked considering their odds.

"Easy," smiled Timmerman.

Craven was already studying the ground all around them as he formed a plan of attack.

"You want to rush them here and now whilst they're stuck?"

It was a tempting prospect, but the enemy had stacks of muskets to hand.

"I don't much fancy charging one hundred muskets over open ground. It will cost us dearly."

"Then what? What would you have us do?"

"There." Craven pointed to where the road narrowed up

ahead into a track with trees on either side, "We go on foot whilst they are occupied trying to free that cart. I do not want them alerted to our presence."

Timmerman looked anxious.

"What is it?"

"They have plenty of horses amongst them. What do we do when they run and go for help? How will we ever get free and clear dragging all that weight ourselves?"

"Then you and your boys stay here. If we force them back this is the only way they can go, and you engage them in the saddle. You make sure not one of them gets past you, do you hear?"

"You know they won't."

"Then let's move whilst we still have time to do this."

Craven rushed back to the others. "Tie up the horses here."

Paget looked horrified.

"Joze will look after them, but there is no time to waste. Let's go."

They were soon on their way, hurrying on along the reverse slope so that they could not be seen, but could get the occasional glimpse of the wagons to know their position and condition. They were all on edge, knowing they were a long way from friendly forces, and nobody would even know where they were if they were to get into trouble. Finally, they reached the position where the road bottlenecked. Craven stopped to assess the scenario. He looked with his spyglass to see the French troops had untethered the horses from one of the other wagons. They were using their brute strength affixed to ropes to heave the stricken wagon free and it was working.

"We don't have long now," gasped Craven as he quickly assessed the scene.

"Ferreira, take your boys onto the far side and get down into cover. You stay hidden until the shooting begins."

The Portuguese Captain hurried on, knowing he'd have to clear the road to get to the cover on the far side quickly.

"Moxy, Caffy, see if you can find a fallen tree, something to block the road with. Nothing fancy, just get it in place."

They went about the work as the remaining few prepared their equipment and got into the best positions they could find. Dense shrubs provided excellent camouflage, and the trees would provide good cover from any musket fire coming back at them. They readied their weapons and adjusted their equipment to get as comfortable as possible to shoot quickly and accurately.

"They will outnumber us, Sir, five to one by my approximation," declared Paget.

"We still have Timmerman and his men."

"But they will not be there when the fight begins. It will only be us."

"Then you must shoot well," smiled Craven, who readied his own rifle, a weapon few ever saw in his hands.

It was not long before the French wagons were on the move once more, and they approached at a steady pace. Craven watched them greedily, as he imagined getting his hands on the precious loot within.

"Moxy, you take the first shot. Every one of you, start with any man on a horse, then officers, then Sergeants, and then any bastard you can see. Do not let any one of them live." He knelt down beside Paget.

"Murdered to a man?" Paget asked worriedly.

"These are not men of the line. Soult would only entrust this job to the sort of men who would murder and steal it all for him in the first place."

"They would do the same to you," insisted Vicenta.

But that partly consoled the Lieutenant who was having doubts about the entire operation, but there was nothing he could say or do about it now.

"Here they come," Craven whispered.

They hunkered down low so they could not be seen, whilst still being able to see the enemy through the foliage before them. They came to a halt not far from the bottleneck of the road as the rider leading the column spotted the obstacle. He cried out as he ordered for several men to come forward to clear it. They sighed in exasperation after just getting back on their journey after the cart had been dislodged from the muddy ditch. The four men who went forward to clear the way did not even take weapons besides the small briquet sabres hanging from their sides. Craven looked to Moxy, gesturing towards the horsemen leading the column, but Moxy already knew what he had to do as he took aim. At that range it was an easy shot for such a skilled marksman, and he did not hesitate to take it. The crack of his rifle echoed out as the man was shot from his horse, and Craven and the others rose up from their positions and took aim. Craven took his shot and struck another from his horse whilst Paget targeted an officer who called to rally his troops, waving his sabre above his head. The American long rifle erupted and with a precise shot to the heart, the officer was downed in one. More fire continued, and then a rippling volley from the far side of the road as Ferreira's riflemen joined them.

It was a brutal opening salvo, but they still had a limited

number of weapons to fire with, and the majority of the French force was still on their feet, taking up muskets and returning fire. Craven hurried to reload his next shot, but as he got up, he could see several Frenchmen at the fallen tree. They were not coming out to hunt them. They were continuing to clear the way.

He spotted an officer giving the orders and fired at him, striking his ball into the man's arm. He dropped his sword but stayed in the saddle, barking his orders to clear the road. A musket ball struck the tree bark besides Craven's face, and he quickly ducked down to go on loading his third shot. In a moment he was back up to fire, but he could see the road was now clear, and the French troops were hurrying to get back onto the wagons. He could see a cloud of smoke in the distance as Timmerman approached from the rear, but this had not been the chaotic mop up operation he had expected it to be.

Craven threw down his rifle and took out his pistol and sword as he broke through the brush. He rushed forward just as the carriages lurched forward. He took aim at one and shot him down as he tried to climb into the moving cart, but he missed his second shot at one atop the wagon who was aiming to fire back at him. Paget shot him down before he could fire at Craven as the Major rushed on with his sword. The wagons were moving at a quick pace, and he could not catch them as he slowed his pace. Paget joined him, sword in hand as they watched the wagons soar off into the distance. Timmerman soon rushed onto the scene.

"What was that?"

"They would not be stopped," replied Craven.

Timmerman cried out angrily. He took aim with his pistol and fired pointlessly at the escaping Frenchmen, now far outside of the reach of his modest weapon. It was as if he were merely howling at the wind in frustration. Craven merely watched the French carts roll away into the distance and did nothing as the others gathered about them.

"What are we waiting for?" Timmerman demanded.

Craven was mentally exhausted and deeply conflicted. He had chosen this path because of the awful events that had led up to the firing squad he had ordered, but now he was starting to wonder what he was even doing.

"We cannot go after them, not with so few horses," insisted Paget.

"We took our chance, and we missed. We failed, but we still have our lives." Matthys tried to put a positive spin on the debacle. Craven turned back to face them all to see most looked as exhausted as he did.

"If we can make our fortune out here in this damned war then we will, but I will tell you one thing for certain. The army needs us, and there will be no treasure to be had if we are not there to support the army we have sweat and bled for all these years. This is over."

"But it's right there!" Timmerman watched the wagons vanish into the distance. Matthys looked stunned and surprised as he realised what Craven was doing and why, but Paget stepped up beside the Major in support of the decision.

"I need that money," growled Timmerman.

"So do we all, far more than you, but there are things more important," insisted Paget.

Timmerman almost wept as he knew he could not do it without them.

"This is just the beginning. Soon we will be fighting our

way across Spain, and Soult will have to flee with everything he has left. We will get another chance," insisted Craven.

"And if we don't?"

"Then march with me to France, and we will take what we are owed, but not from the people of that land like he did. We will march all the way to his home and take it from him with our own hands if we must."

"I won't end this war a poor man, Craven."

"Better a poor man than a dead one," replied Paget.

"We will find our riches, but it is not today," insisted Craven.

Timmerman breathed a sigh of relief as the tension was lifted, and he had come to terms with the fact that it could not be done.

"Come on, let's get back to this war."

"I always knew you'd be the end of me, Craven, but not like this," he smiled.

CHAPTER 11

"It was the right thing to do." They approached the army as it made encampment for another day, and Matthys could see how conflicted Craven looked, but he shrugged it off as that was not on his mind at all.

"I know. it's just good to be back."

They rode calmly on.

"The Craven I used to know would never have said that. He would have gone after those wagons to the end of the world even if it killed him."

"I'm not sure I ever had that much spirit."

"Oh, yes, you did."

"I gave up on those wagons because it was the wrong time, but I will try again. I won't return to England a poor man."

"Nor I."

"You? You would want riches?"

"Do you know all the good which may be achieved with money?"

"I can think of a lot," he agreed.

"They say Napoleon lives like a king even if he does not call himself one. In palaces dripping with gold and jewels the likes of which would make King George blush," declared Matthys, as he had now become the treasure hunter.

"And you would relieve him of it?"

"That is the nature of their revolution, is it not? I would spend that money more honestly than that tyrant ever has."

"Perhaps you should be Emperor, then?" Craven laughed.

"Imagine what someone like me could do in those shoes? All that power and a will to do good by the people, not squander everything the country has on war."

"Do you think the French people want war and conquest, Sir?" Paget asked.

"I think they want whatever Napoleon tells them they want."

"I don't know why they love him so much," pondered Paget.

"Because you have never lived as a poor man under a French king," replied Matthys, causing Craven to laugh again.

They soon caught a glimpse of the rest of the Salfords and their encampment. They arrived to a warm welcome by all except Gamboa, who had a fearful look upon his face.

"What is it?" Craven asked.

"You, Sir, are to report to Wellington immediately, and Captain Ferreira also."

"What is this regarding?"

"I do not know, Sir, but Major Spring said it was of great importance."

Craven sighed, as he was eager to get out of the saddle and

get a good meal in him, but he gestured for Ferreira to go on with him.

"Do you need my assistance, Sir?"

"No, Mr Paget. Stay here. I want you to oversee anyone who comes looking for instruction. For those were our orders, and I am sure we are about to get an earful for leaving it to others."

They rode on just as he saw a party of troops gathering to receive their training with the sword and bayonet. It was a great sight to see and a pleasant reminder that Craven had done the right thing when he abandoned the treasure hunt.

"How much did it kill you to see how close we came to being rich men? To watch it ride off into the distance?" Ferreira asked.

"I won't lie it was a shame, but I don't worry about it half as much as you think. What good is wealth if we do not live long enough to spend it? We will get plenty more chances to fill our pockets with gold, but for now we have to see this army to victory."

"Do you still believe it can be done?"

"If Napoleon came down here and threw everything at us, we would be washed away into the sea, never to return. But rumour is that the Emperor calls troops back to France for another endeavour, and so yes."

"I am not sure if that is comforting or not, to know he gathers his forces to strike someplace else."

"Perhaps the monarchists are making noises again, or perhaps he thinks he can finally cross the Channel and invade England or go East and expand his borders once more?"

"Could it be England? Could he finally be making the

crossing?" Ferreira was concerned, as he knew what that would mean for his own country.

"I don't know," sighed Craven, "They say the Royal Navy's strength will never allow it to happen, but it's a short jump to Dover."

"Why doesn't he come down here himself and finish this job?"

"I imagine he has his eye on greater prizes than Portugal and Spain, but he is a fool to think so. Wellington will gnaw away at the belly of his Empire from here."

Soon enough they reached a house that had become Wellington's headquarters and were shown through with little wait. Wellington looked exasperated as they approached, which made them both concerned that the war had somehow turned against their favour. The door was shut behind them so that it was only the General and Major Spring.

"Major Craven, an accusation has been brought to my attention which is of grave concern," declared Wellington.

Craven shrugged as he imagined they were about to get yelled at for not remaining at their posts to give instruction as ordered.

"I am not sure you have grasped the seriousness of this situation, Craven," added Spring.

"Witnesses allege that you conducted a firing squad and executed a soldier of this army," Wellington continued.

"Is this coming from Colonel Blakeney and Major Rooke?" Craven replied angrily.

"It doesn't matter where I received this information from, Major. It matters whether it is true, well, is it?"

Craven sighed and nodded in agreement.

"Why? Why would you be so stupid?" Wellington crashed his hand down on his desk before lying back in his chair and groaning in pain.

"Sir, the man's offences were grave. He raped a local woman and my men bore witness to it, Captain Ferreira himself, Sir," insisted Craven as he defended their actions.

"And so that man would have been hanged after a short investigation, and rightfully so."

"What then is the difference? For the result would have been the same."

"I cannot have officers executing soldiers for crimes without evidence, Major. A man must see a fair trial!"

"And the girl he raped? Was she treated fairly?" Ferreira yelled.

Wellington slammed his fist down once more as he sprang up onto his feet.

"Damn it, I will not be spoken to like that!"

But he soon sat back down as he did sympathise for the woman.

"Will she be all right?"

"Not for a long time."

Wellington sighed as he was put in a difficult spot.

"Why did you not come to me?" he asked rhetorically, for they all knew the reason why. Craven was hot tempered and with little patience, not unlike the General himself.

"This was Blakeney and Rooke, wasn't it, Sir?" Craven asked.

"Yes, and now I must appease them. For they were right to bring it to my attention and I cannot do nothing, or I will lose control of this whole bloody army. I can save you a court martial,

Craven, because I have that power and because we are on the eve of battle. But you cannot go unpunished, not just to appease Colonel Blakeney, but because this army must know discipline, even you."

Craven sighed, knowing there was no fighting it.

"Major Craven, the responsibility for this is yours and yours alone. You have conducted yourself with many admirable qualities throughout this campaign and your promotion was well earned, but also through your own actions have you forced my hand to now do what I must. From now on you will be a Captain once more."

"A demotion, Sir?" Craven asked angrily.

"You never even wanted it to begin with," protested Spring.

"Until I did. It meant a lot to the men who I lead, and you would take it away from me?"

"You take it away from yourself," replied Wellington wearily.

"Will that be all, Sir?"

"It is."

"Permission to be dismissed?"

"Of course, but, Craven?"

"Yes, Sir?"

"I need you in this fight, Craven. Do not give me another reason to have to discipline you. For in time many might wonder if you are fit to serve in this army, but I know otherwise. I know that no one will fight harder for England when the time comes. Do not do anything more to compromise your position here."

"Yes, Sir."

They walked out to find Blakeney and Rooke watching

from a distance with glee as they muttered and giggled amongst themselves. Craven was close to boiling point with rage, but Ferreira took his arm.

"Leave them be. No good can come of it."

Craven grumbled angrily, knowing his Portuguese friend was correct, but he did not take his eyes from his two accusers for a few moments. He wanted to tear them apart, and he wanted them to know it. Ferreira finally dragged him away as they went back to their horses.

"It doesn't mean anything. You will be back up to Major soon enough. Wellington had to be seen to do something, and this is on me also," insisted Ferreira as they got into the saddles.

"How do your figure that?"

"I was the one that dragged that man out. I was the one who whipped up a storm. I was the one who struck him, and I was the one who prepared a firing squad without question."

"Because it was the right thing to do, and everyone knows it."

"But we knew eyes were on us and we knew those bastards were watching and waiting for us to make a mistake. We should have been smarter than that."

Craven shrugged.

"I won't apologise for being what we are."

"It could have been far worse. The punishment, I mean."

Craven knew it to be true as he could have lost everything. Only his worth and commitment to the army had saved him. They rode back to find Paget eagerly conducting drills. Several others fought with singlesticks and padded sticks to represent their bayonets. Few doubted the worth of the training any longer, but Craven was surprised to find Le Marchant in the audience of those watching from the sidelines.

"A Captain once more?" he smiled as Craven joined him.

"News travels quickly."

"I knew this decision before you did. You have a remarkable ability to find yourself in trouble, not only with the enemy, but with your allies also," smiled Le Marchant.

"Blakeney and Rooke are not my allies," seethed Craven.

"Oh, but they are, and the sooner you understand that the better. We will never like every one of our countrymen, and they will never all like us, but we do still fight for the same cause and wear the same uniform. We must find some way to go on, no matter how much we hate one another, for we have important work to do."

Craven sighed. The General was right, but he still didn't like it.

"You are lucky to have a friend in Wellington. Any other commanding officer would have rung you out for those charges."

"Because I have a use."

"That much is certain. The army is lucky to have you, but then you are lucky to have the army, for what would you be otherwise?"

Craven shrugged. The alternative was as he had already lived it, and he never wanted to go back to those days.

"Colonel Blakeney will not stop coming for you."

"I can't duel with them. You know I can't."

"No, that would be foolish."

"Then what do you suggest?"

"You can keep butting heads with them and try to win the battle, or you can prove to them that their perception of you is wrong. Prove to them that you deserve a place here."

"You ask the impossible, for they have made their decision on me."

"I hear Major Timmerman was once your greatest enemy, and that now the very same man defended you before Wellington. Timmerman is a far more formidable adversary than Blakeney or Rooke will ever be. You have already achieved the impossible, and so for you this new task will be easy."

Craven shook his head in disbelief.

"You do not need to use your strength and your sword to defeat every obstacle before you, Craven."

Craven chuckled at the prospect.

"That is funny coming from a man who insisted the army adopt swords that could cleave a horse in two," he joked.

"Speaking of swords, did you do as I advised and purchase a sword of the type I devised?"

Craven shook his head.

"You go to war with that little thing when you could have a fine sabre," jabbed Le Marchant.

Craven dared not bring up the moment his parry was almost forced through by a heavy sabre cut recently as it would only add more weight to the General's argument.

"I can't say I have the money with which to purchase one, nor the chance to do so, for there are no good makers of good British swords out here," lamented Craven, for he had no respect for Portuguese made swords. In his eyes the only good swords the Portuguese troops used were the ones sent from England, which were exported in great quantity to all of their allies.

"There are many fine smiths in Spain, and soon enough

we will gain access to them as the army progresses."

"I hope so."

"Keep on at it, Craven," replied Le Marchant as he walked away.

"I always do," smiled Craven.

He turned back to the training party to get a better assessment of them, for he intended to take Le Marchant's words to heart. There were some things in life and in the army he could not change, but a body of soldiers eager to learn with weapons in hand, this was something he could make an impact on.

"Halt!"

Everyone did as they were ordered to do.

"Mr Paget here is a fine teacher. I know, because I taught him everything that he knows!"

Paget did not protest as there was certainly a lot of truth to it.

"Except how to shoot!" Moxy yelled, which drew a great deal of laughter, and Craven enjoyed it, too.

"All right, all right." He called for silence, "There are some in the army who believe that skill at arms with the sword is only for the cavalry, and that skill with the bayonet is not required at all. That it is merely a barbaric hold over from before we had muskets and rifles, and that men need only courage and strength to succeed with such a tool. I hope by now you all realise that could not be further from the truth. A great many battles have been decided with cold steel, and those who are better with it will triumph. Let us see then if Mr Paget has taught you the skills you need to face the enemy and win!"

He took off his sword belt and pulled a singlestick from

Paget's hands.

"Who will face me? Who believes they can land a blow on me?"

"I will!" roared a stout young Private from Ireland.

He looked fresh and farm strong from having worked a labour-intensive job for the few years he had been a man.

"Come forward!"

The Irishman had a padded stick in his hands to represent the musket and fixed bayonet.

"If you can land the point of your bayonet or the butt of your musket on me before I land a blow against your head or torso, you win, understand?"

"Yes, Sir," nodded the man excitedly.

The two came to their guards as everyone else watched on with great anticipation.

"Begin!"

The man edged forward, and Craven snapped a quick rotational cut against the man's lead forearm, striking at the bone. The burly Irishman took it like an ox and smiled back.

"Head or torso you said," he declared.

"Yes, I did," smirked Craven.

He lashed another cut in against the man's head, to find it was parried away and a thrust came back for him. He parried it aside, but the Irishman soared forward relentlessly, swinging the butt in a large horizontal stroke for his face. Craven bent his body and arched away so that the butt of the stick flashed past his eyes. He backed away and nodded in approval. His opponent did not just fight with strength, but also precision. He had listened to Paget and implemented what he had been taught. Now he initiated the attack with a single thrust, but as Craven lifted his sword to parry the blow, he realised it was merely a deception. His singlestick met nothing but air as the Irishman retracted his own stick before thrusting in again.

Craven's response was quick, but once again his opponent retracted and made another thrust until finally, they parted again. It was Craven's turn to make an assault now as his opponent caught his breath. He lashed out with another cut towards the Irishman's arms, but this time he targeted he knuckles of his left hand, giving them a good wrap. The man gave out a cry in pain as the muzzle instinctively fell from his hands from the pain surging through his hand.

Craven rotated the blade quickly as if to deal a tremendous blow onto his opponent's head who could no longer defend in that moment. But the stick struck with the tiniest of force as Craven pulled it short, landing with just enough power to signify a hit, but not enough to do harm.

A cheer rang out as the audience loved every second of the martial display, but Craven soon called them to silence once more.

"He fought well! Fight like that, and there will not be a Frenchman who can stand before you!"

Another cheer rang out even more loudly than the last as Craven returned the stick to Paget.

"Good work, Lieutenant. As you were."

Paget could not hope to hear sweeter words. It meant he had Craven's approval in the thing he cared most about in life, the art of defence. Craven turned to leave.

"Major Craven, Sir?"

Craven hesitated before stopping.

"What did Lord Wellington want with you?"

"Nothing of consequence, but it is Captain Craven," he replied before going on his way.

Paget's heart sank, and he looked distraught. He wanted to press for a reason why but dared not. He did not have to wait for long. Ferreira came to explain, knowing Paget would not stop hounding them until he had some answers and wanting to save himself such an experience.

"A demotion? How can Lord Wellington demote such a man as Craven? We would not even still be able to go on fighting this war if it was not for men like him," declared Paget angrily.

"We put a man to a firing squad. There were always going to be consequences for that, but don't you worry about Craven. He could have become Major anytime in the last two years, and if he wants it again, he will get it."

CRAVEN'S WAR – THE FINAL CHANCE

CHAPTER 12

Morning soon came. The army around them had not moved and would not do so until the following day. Craven was up at the crack of dawn, eager to make himself busy as he warmed his hands beside a fire.

"We do not move today, Sir?" Paget joined him.

"The roads cannot move for soldiers. We must wait for them to clear, but we will be on our way soon enough."

The others slowly began to arise, and it was Amyn who was next to join them, happy at the sight of the fire. Craven often wondered how a Mameluke survived in the wet and cold they were facing, and yet he always then felt foolish, remembering how cold the desert could be.

"You train them well," declared Amyn.

"Someone has to." Craven was still angry with how little the army valued such experience.

"Do your people often practice with the sword?" Paget

asked him.

"Yes, very often, and with the spear and with the bow," he replied proudly.

"Le Marchant certainly thinks highly of you and your ways. If he had his way, we would all be carrying crooked scimitars like that." Craven gestured towards the kilij sword the Mameluke carried.

Scimitar was the name by which many foreign sabres had become known, and even some British-made ones, but mostly it referred to the short and flat blade the Ottomans and Mamelukes were so famous for using.

"Then he is a wise man. For every cut should be such that it can slice a man in two."

Craven smiled as he was reminded of his arguments about sword designs with the General.

"Why is it, Sir, that we have such a diverse variety of sword types, even within our army? Our officers carry both straight and curved swords, of light and heavy weight. Our light cavalrymen carry their plain sabres with a single bow for protection, and the heavy cavalry have such a long and straight blade with a formidable ward iron of flat steel. Why do we have so many types?"

"Because two men will never agree on what makes the best sword, and sometimes they can both be right at the same time," chuckled Craven.

"Can it not be calculated scientifically?"

"Not when swordsmanship is as much an art as a science. You can decide the qualities you want best in a sword, and then choose which succeeds best in those tests. That sword you carry, it is the fastest a long cut and thrust sword can move. It prioritises speed at the tip over all else. Amyn's scimitar is far shorter, and though of the same weight, it carries more of that weight forward and so cannot change direction with the same speed but can cut with three times the ferocity. Who are we to say which is the best path?"

Paget did not look convinced.

"Think of it in terms of ships. Some ships are light and fast so they might deliver their cargo rapidly. Others have vastly more capacity and will deliver a far greater load but much more slowly. Others still, such as a good warship prioritise gunnery and dedicate a great deal of their payload to cannon, ammunition, and powder. But then which guns do you choose? Long guns for engaging at a range or short guns for devastating your adversaries up close? Which are more important to you? Bow chasers so that you may go after and pursue a vessel? Or a double or triple deck on the broadside for a brawl? We have not even yet considered ammunition, nor the thickness of the hull to make the vessel resilient. A ship cannot be all things. It cannot be fast, heavily armed, and also capable of carrying a great payload. A sword is no different."

"But the sword which strikes first is better, is it not?"

Craven laughed as he had not really listened to any of it.

"Never change, Mr Paget, for you are a constant that we all need in our lives," he smiled.

"Did Lord Wellington really demote you, Sir?"

"He did," replied Craven calmly, having come to terms with it.

"It's not fair, Sir."

"No, but it is not the worst thing ever done to a man, and when we are climbing the walls of Badajoz, it won't matter whether I am Major or Captain, only that I am there."

"I will fight to get you back to your standing, Sir, just as you have fought for me."

"Thank you." Craven was sincere, for it meant the world to know he had friends watching his back and carrying him forward.

"What now then, Sir?"

"Our future it set. The slow creep on towards Badajoz goes on. We keep training the troops until it is our time to go at the walls of that fortress."

"And then all of Spain will open to us?"

"That is what they say. The two keys to Spain, we have one, and the other is within our reach. It could change everything. No more skulking about in Portugal, but on to glory."

"Glory, Sir? Is that what you seek?"

"That is what we need, for it is tied to all that matters. Our survival, our success, the freedom of the people of these lands, and our chance to find riches. Everything relies on the great successes of this army."

"Then all of this training we are doing, it is in fact of great importance, and not merely a chore set upon us?"

"I have dedicated my life to the art of defence, and it is through that knowledge and skill that we are all here today. If every soldier we instruct gains a small fraction of skill from our work, then it will make a difference. When a battle hangs in the balance, as men battle it out with bayonets. When the line must be bolstered. When our lads dart in against the enemy. When the breach of a fortress is battled over and every single swing of a sword, every parry, and every thrust of a bayonet can mean the difference between success and failure, the training we have bestowed upon them can be the difference between winning and losing a battle. In turn a battle won or lost can change the whole course of the war."

Paget was stunned, realising just how much weight lay on his shoulders with the responsibility he had to those he taught.

"Here they come," declared Craven.

Paget looked up in horror to see dozens of soldiers flocking to them for further instruction. He looked deeply nervous now as he felt the pressure which Craven had outlined.

"Nothing has changed," insisted Craven.

"But it has. I never truly appreciated the importance of our work here, and now that I know, it is like a ball and chain about my ankle."

"Would you rather not have known?"

"Yes, and no. It would have been better to not have known, but I also know that the things we do not know can get us killed."

"You have nothing to fear, for you know how to do this. You know how to fight, and you know how to teach others to fight. You can do no harm here, only good."

Paget breathed a sigh of relief as it helped to hear it.

"Keep doing what you have been doing, and not only can you help these men to success, but you may save some of their lives, and give them the tools to save the lives of others."

"That is a lot of responsibility."

"As an officer that is your duty every single day."

Paget looked a little dumbfounded as he realised what he was doing now was nothing as scary as leading soldiers into battle, and that calmed him significantly. They watched as dozens more soldiers arrived to begin training. Many were familiar faces as men who they had taught before. Soon enough there were more than one hundred soldiers gathered to begin their training. A stack of sticks lay nearby which could be used in place of swords and muskets.

Craven and his associates no longer had to waste time convincing the troops of why their training was necessary. They eagerly soaked up every word they said and looked forward to the training. With every day they got more enthusiastic as the training continued and the army drew closer to Badajoz. For hours the men trained without even stopping for water, enthusiastically going through drills whilst others took it in turns practicing their skills with the singlesticks and padded sticks.

At noon two-dozen officers approached to see for themselves how the training was progressing and assess its value with their own eyes.

"Keep working them," Craven ordered Paget as he went to greet the party.

"The men still flock to you and volunteer for these duties, remarkable," declared Le Marchant. He was overjoyed at the sight of such enthusiasm for the exercise for cold steel weapons. The officers gossiped amongst themselves as they argued over the methods and usefulness of what they were seeing.

"Colonel Blakeney, what do you think of all of this?" Le Marchant asked.

All the officers were silenced as they watched on with great intrigue to hear the arguments.

"Captain Craven is not fit to conduct the training of these fine men."

He put a great emphasis on Craven's new rank and the

demotion which he had worked so hard to achieve. Yet he was clearly not happy with that punishment as he wanted Wellington to go further. Gasps echoed out from a number of those around him as they were harsh words indeed. Craven looked to Le Marchant as if to beg his permission to fight back. For he would not take any more risks in that regard, and that was the only reason the Colonel dared speak out and offend him so, as he treated Craven as if he were a bear chained to a pole. A ferocious animal that could be poked and prodded from a distance. He aimed to utterly humiliate him before the entire army. But Le Marchant smirked as he had set a trap of his own.

"Captain Craven has been punished for his mistakes, but his ability to fight and to teach others to fight was never in doubt, nor was his honour. You, Sir, question the Captain's honour," declared Le Marchant boldly.

Blakeney was stunned by the direct assault of the General and could not find his words. Le Marchant only continued with his barrage as swiftly and violently as he swung his sabre.

"You, Sir, call into question the honour of a great man, and Captain Craven would be quite within his rights to demand satisfaction. What's more I would be his second, for I would not stand to see a good fighting man disparaged from the sidelines by a lesser man."

Blakeney's face went pale as he realised the General had not just given his support for a challenge, but he had released him from the chain which kept Craven from lashing out at him. With the General's support, he could make a challenge without angering Wellington. Craven was enjoying every second of it as he watched the cavalry officer's plan unfold beautifully. This was no mere inspection by officers of the army. It was an assassination of Blakeney and the despicable hold he held over Craven. The other officers marvelled at the scene, with their noses to the gossip trough and delighting in the discomfort before them. They eagerly waited to see if they would see blood this day. Blakeney had no words, knowing he was now at Craven's mercy.

"Well, Captain, what do you say?" Le Marchant gave all the power into the situation over to Craven.

Craven remained silent for a while, letting his adversary sweat for an uncomfortable amount of time. Finally, he broke the silence, and did so loudly and boldly for all to hear.

"It is beyond belief that an officer of this army, who wears the same uniform as I, who marches towards the same battle as I, an officer who should be my brother; a man like that would call into question my honour and my dedication to these fine soldiers and this fine army. I will have satisfaction," he declared, enjoying every second of Blakeney's discomfort.

A cheer rang out from the men he had been instructing all morning, but Craven raised his hand to call for silence. He was not done, and he went on.

"However! I would not ever want to rob this army of a fellow officer on the eve of battle, and so if the Major was prepared to offer a full and thorough apology, I would be willing to consider this matter settled!"

Blakeney was stunned and shaken.

"What will it be, Colonel?" Le Marchant asked.

"Well…I…I…" he fumbled before stopping to regain his composure and started again, "I am sorry for this misunderstanding, and I offer my complete apology. For I misspoke and was quite out of line."

"Captain, do you accept this apology?"

"Yes, but of course I would consider the apology hollow, and the matter re-opened should I hear that the gentleman has repeated any of the terrible things he has said of my character in the days, weeks, and years ahead."

"Quite right, then this matter is closed?" Le Marchant pressed for Blakeney to agree to the terms that would hold him to not pursuing Craven any further. Craven could now justifiably call him to a duel anytime he felt he had been wronged.

"Quite so. It was my mistake, and I apologise for my part in it. This war is what matters to each and every one of us, and that is where our attentions must be placed," added Blakeney as he tried to save face, "I must be on my way to see to the morning duties," he added, marching on with his tail between his legs, and Craven watching with delight.

"Thank you," he declared earnestly to the cavalry General who had overcome his adversary without ever having drawn a blade and only his wit.

"Men like that have no place in war. Perhaps he might be of use back home in the recruiting and training of soldiers, but I have my doubts."

Craven chuckled along as he knew it was true. It was made all the funnier for they both knew there were many more like Blakeney, and not one thing they could do to change it. Craven took a deep breath in and out as he relaxed. He felt a great weight be lifted from his shoulders. Blakeney would not dare cause trouble now he had Le Marchant breathing down his neck.

"You did me a great service."

"Good, then you can do me one in return."

"Anything."

"I want you to teach my boys. The Heavy Brigade I command."

"You would have me teach them the use of the sword when they have you?" Craven gasped.

"I am a cavalryman, Craven, and whilst I bested you in the saddle, when the battle went to the ground you were a terror. There are times when a cavalryman must fight on foot, over difficult terrain, through the little towns and villages of this land, and should a man ever lose his horse, an unfortunate incident which is sometimes unavoidable. When my boys find themselves in these encounters I realise now that I have not prepared them fully for what that might mean. But you, Craven, that is where you shine. Teach my boys the way of defence on foot. Will you do that for me?"

"Of course, I will. It is the least I can do, and it would be pleasure. However, I am not sure your boys will be too eager to learn from an infantryman."

The cavalry had always thought of themselves as superior, and they also saw the sword as their defining weapon, with little respect for how the infantry practiced.

"They might not respect you from afar, but they respect what they can see before them. They will soon see the way."

"Then by all means."

Le Marchant gestured to one of his men standing nearby, and in just a few moments there were dozens of heavy cavalry officers and sergeants approaching.

"You planned this well," smiled Craven, realising Le Marchant had thought of everything.

Craven looked over to Paget and the others who went on instructing the infantry. He was content he could leave them to go on as he took on this new responsibility. He was relieved to see the men of the Heavy Brigade brought their own singlesticks, with several sergeants carrying bundles under their arms. Craven approached and took one to inspect himself. It was of a heavy construction, fifty percent heavier than what they typically used, and better suited to representing the long straight sword of the heavy cavalry that every one of them wore.

"May I?" he asked the Sergeant who he had retrieved the singlestick from, as he now marvelled at the man's cold steel.

"Yes, Sir."

The Sergeant drew out the blade and handed it over without hesitation. It was big, three inches longer than his infantry sword and the much-curved sabre designed and beloved by Le Marchant. It had all the forward mass of the light cavalry sabre but was overall larger, not just in the blade but also with a very protective gilt made crudely from a dish of iron protecting the top of the hand. It was most akin to the Highland broadsword in size, protection, and handling. A brutish weapon, and yet not all that clumsy, considering its formidable size.

He began to swing it about to test its handling. It was crude to what he was accustomed, but he could understand how it could do good work in strong and capable hands, which the soldiers of the heavy cavalry certainly were. They recruited the tallest and strongest, and mounted them on the largest horses with the largest swords used in the British army. They were a brute force instrument, a shock troop.

"With a sword like this, one might wonder if you ever meant to cut a man at all or rather bludgeon him to death," joked Craven.

Some of the men laughed as they enjoyed their reputation

as brawlers, but others looked insulted, as if Craven was undermining their weapons and their skills. The officers amongst them carried swords with far more elaborate honeysuckle-like bowl guard swords, but with the same blade and proportions they were functionally identical weapons to the brutish-looking troopers' sword. He handed the sword back and made the same movements and rotations with the singlestick to test its handling. It was lighter than the cold steel, but still formidable, such that it could easily knock a man out cold with a smart blow to the head.

"I am surprised you do not have all of these men with your fine sabres by now," declared Craven to Le Marchant.

"If only it would be permitted. Alas, I have pressed for the sabre to be used by all in the saddle, but the army will not always see reason, and a great many of these men are quite fond of their swords. And if they wield them with pride and skill. then who am I to take them away?"

Craven nodded in agreement. He could see the Heavy Brigade had a great love and respect for their General, but he had not yet earnt even a fraction of it, and so he knew he had work to do as they watched him with suspicion and doubt.

"I am not here to show you how to fight. I know you can do that. With General Le Marchant seeing to your training, I have no doubt you are better in the saddle than I will ever be. I truly believe that, but now please respect what I have to say when I am absolutely certain that on a battle on foot there is not a man amongst you who could best me."

Groans of disapproval rang out, and that made Craven smile.

"However, I do not expect you to take my word on this

matter. You have no reason to do so, but I will change that here and now. I will fight three of you, each one-to-one single good strong blow, and so the three finest and boldest amongst you please step forward. And when I am triumphant over all three of you, then you will believe me."

Le Marchant chuckled as he was loving every minute of it, for he could not lose. If Craven won the challenge, then he would prove why he was worthy of instructing them. And if the cavalrymen won, then it would underline the quality of the instruction and training he himself had imparted onto them.

"I will challenge you, Sir," declared the Sergeant whose sword he had inspected.

The man looked to be a veteran of a decade or more and evidently took the pride of his regiment and of the skill of his own arm seriously. As one who carried the singlesticks, Craven suspected he might be a sword master to the regiment. He took off his sword belt and came forward with one of the singlesticks. Even those training with Paget had stopped to witness the contest, for the heavy cavalry were famed for their ferocity and all were eager to see if Craven could resist them.

The Sergeant took up his guard with his sword extended out parallel to the ground and the tip of his sword held well back. His feet were close together and quite upright, and his left hand held as if it clutched the reins of his horse. It was how almost every cavalryman held himself when fighting on foot and always looked so amusing to anyone who dedicated any serious time to practice on foot. Yet he looked strong and confident. He came forward a few paces but did not give away any openings.

Craven moved his arm across to change his guard from one side to another, a deception to bait his man to make an attack, and he did so as if by command. Craven took the heavy cut on a hanging guard, returning his own by rotating at the wrist and cutting down with a downward with a diagonal cut, the cut called cut one, which all swordsmen were accustomed to. The Sergeant parried it with ease, but the blow was not the one Craven intended to strike with, and he was not done. He turned his hand and drove the point in around the Sergeant's guard, jamming the completely rigid ash stave into the man's chest with enough force to make him wince and gasp. Singlesticks were only ever intended to be a safe cutting implement and struck remarkably hard on the thrust, yet nobody protested. As soldiers they must expect to have to counter the point, especially when facing the French who favoured it far more so than the English. Le Marchant clapped at the display as the Sergeant saluted gracefully in defeat before another man stepped up to challenge Craven.

This time an eager Lieutenant who looked much more spry and eager to impress if not show off. They each came to their guards as the Lieutenant bobbed his sword about from side to side and up and down. These were the sort of motions some men learnt by instinct after a lot of practice. They used their constant rhythms to be unpredictable to their opponent, so that they could never predict when and where an attack would come from. It unsettled many fencers, but Craven had dealt with countless fighters like him, and so he did not wait to be attacked this time. He feint a blow to the man's head and then feinted with a seemingly even stronger blow to the other side of his face. He dropped down into a longer lunge, cracking his heavy singlestick into the man's thigh with such power his legs went out from under him, and he crashed down onto the soft ground.

The young man looked stunned, for he never imagined he was even in range to be struck. Once again, Le Marchant clapped, but none of his heavy cavalrymen did, as they were frustrated at being humiliated.

A Captain stepped forward to be the third and last challenge against Craven.

"Come on, Leighton!" roared another in support of the Captain.

He was clearly popular with the men and officers alike as they all pinned their hopes on him now. Captain Leighton was a tall and strong man who moved with grace. Craven imagined he would make a fine fencer, and he did indeed relax into a position more akin to Craven's, though he still looked awkward in it, as if it had been learnt through experience rather than training. Craven feinted with a cut, launching a cut at his lead leg, but it was merely a test. He knew the man would be expecting it, having seen what he had done to the last cavalryman.

A thunderous blow came down towards Craven's head, but he was ready for it and backed away under a strong guard. A cheer rang out as if Leighton had gained the upper hand, but Craven knew he was still in control. Leighton lashed a blow towards his arm and then another from underneath at the same target, as if he were toying with Craven, and his audience loved it. Leighton then made a feint with a cut to Craven's inside before lowering himself into a lunge and reached to cut Craven's flank. But Craven dropped his stick off Leighton's, who in turn tried to strike around at Craven's face. Craven lifted his basket, took the blow on a hanging guard, and took a leap forward. In doing so, his left hand reached through under his parry and took hold of his opponent's singlestick at the basket, locking it in place. He took another pace again as Leighton tried to back away, but Craven now looped his left arm around the singlestick. He locked it entirely in place before raising his stick up as if to strike his defenceless opponent on the crown of his head, but as he did, he froze in place.

"Do you yield?"

"I do," he replied, thankful to not have his head split.

Le Marchant clapped once more, but still nothing from his men who looked stunned and a little disillusioned. Craven let go of Leighton, and he went back to the others with his pride dealt a heavy blow.

"There is no shame in losing like you did. I told you when you came here that I am better at this than you, and now you know it to be true. I know for certain that the General here will have ensured you are all fine horsemen and ferocious cavalrymen. I should know because I have crossed swords with him myself. He has given you the tools and ability to be the best you can be in the saddle, but when the time comes that you do not have a horse beneath you, you will be glad of another set of skills, and those are skills I can teach you. So do not be disheartened. There is nothing to feel shame for, but the very opposite. You will leave here as even finer and more terrifying swordsmen than you were yesterday. How does that sound?"

"If you can teach me what you did there so that I might do it to the French, then I salute you, Sir," declared Leighton.

Cheers and clapping rang out from his comrades as they realised the opportunity they had before them. Craven had won them over, and Le Marchant was as impressed by his strategy as Craven had been at the trap he himself had set for Blakeney.

"Pick up your sticks. We have some good work to do!"

Craven roared.

They all hurried to take off their sword belts and join in the training with great enthusiasm as Paget could be heard calling his students to get back to their exercises.

For four hours Craven trained the heavy cavalrymen who were in good spirits and listened intently to everything Craven had to offer. He moulded and adopted the skills they had to make them a fierce bunch of broadswordsmen. When all was done, and they were dripping in sweat, Craven called them to a halt and had them gather around. There was a sense of achievement in their faces, which elevated not just them but everyone around who watched on.

"Fine work, all of you. I know being a cavalryman you feel above us in the infantry, and you are indeed above us, by the height of a horse!" jested Craven, drawing laughter, "We all fight to the same end, and every success of the cavalry is a success for the infantry, and vice versa. I wish you every luck in the coming days and weeks."

A cheer rang out as Le Marchant strode up to Craven. He carried a sheathed cavalry sabre in his hands, but it was not his own which was still hanging from his side.

"Captain Craven, please take this as gift of gratitude for the time and patience you have shown us here today."

Another cheer rang out as he handed over the sword. It was an officer's type of the light cavalry pattern, but it was quite plain in decoration, and yet special in other ways. The long beaked and faceted pommel was truly stunning. As he drew out the blade just a few inches, he could see the inscription on the deep fuller of the blade. It read 'Gill, Warranted Never to Fail.'

"A fine gift!"

Paget looked over Craven's shoulder. For he himself carried a sword made by Gill of Birmingham, which were some of the finest and strongest swords made in all of England, if not the world. A warranted blade cost twice that of a regular one and coming from such a reputable maker was quite the statement. Craven ripped the rest of the blade from the steel scabbard and swung several cuts and rotations. It was sublime, being a tad lighter in the blade than the troopers' versions, and the long, elongated pommel made it balance a little closer to the hand than those cleavers.

"It is beautiful," declared Craven. He was stunned by the fantastic gift.

"He was a fine man who came to Portugal with that sword to serve England, and it was a shame he never got a chance to use it, but I can assure you he would have been overjoyed to know it went to the hands of a master of the sword such as yourself."

"Then I will carry it to Spain and then onto France!" He thrust the blade triumphantly into the air and drew the roar of the excited crowd who were elated by the scene.

CHAPTER 13

On the army marched, away from the paradise of Castelo de Vide and on towards the hellish fortress of Badajoz. It was the final leg on the march to the Southern crossing point into Spain and the second so-called key to the country. Anticipation and excitement were felt amongst them all, but equally there was a sense of dread. Not a soldier amongst them imagined it would be an easy affair or obstacle to overcome, but the prospect of victory and an advance into Spain kept spirits and morale very high.

They were marching to victory. That is what the senior officers of the army told them, and yet Craven could not help think of what Le Marchant had shared with him. Those in command were not confident of victory at all, and in fact many were merely counting down the days to defeat so that they might return home. He could not share this information with anyone but his closest friends and confidents. It would undermine morale so severely they might fulfil the bleak prophecy that those naysaying officers felt in their hearts. Craven knew a fighter needed to be confident in their chance of victory to stand any chance of achieving it, and he was not about to rob the army of that confidence.

Craven looked back at the force he commanded with pride and confidence in their ability to fight and support him no matter what. As he gazed upon them, he realised one issue still needed to be resolved as he noticed Matthys looking back at Amyn with resentment. Even after all the Mameluke had done for them, Matthys could not trust nor find any love in his heart for the man. He did indeed still look like an outsider amongst them, a foreigner so far removed from their customs. He was unapologetic in that fact as he so proudly clung to his roots, despite the devastating loss of his people. Craven sighed, knowing the peaceful day was about to come to an end. He had to attempt to resolve the clash before they went into battle once more, and so he rode back to be beside the Sergeant, one of his oldest friends.

"Is everything all right?"

Craven shrugged as he tried to find the words.

"Whatever it is, you can share it with me," insisted Matthys.

"We march to a great battle, one which I suspect will test us to our very limits, and I would have us as one, united and strong."

"Are we not?" Matthys proclaimed as if it were not in doubt.

"We are not. Not quite. You still harbour ill thoughts towards Amyn," declared Craven bluntly.

"I do," admitted Matthys.

"Why? After all he has done for us?"

"Because I have seen who and what he is," seethed Matthys.

"You've seen what I am, too."

"But you are not beyond saving, and perhaps you are already saved."

"And he is not?"

"He is still a savage."

Craven shook his head in disbelief.

"He was a slave trader."

"Was, and I was many things in a past life, but what are we now? What are you? Where is your forgiveness? Where is your compassion?"

"You would question that of me?" Matthys scowled.

"I would, and so should you. You look at a man and see him as something lesser, and I have never seen that from you before. I think you forget yourself. He has done more than enough to prove he has a place here. He has done it ten times over, but still, you will not open your arms to him, yet you will forgive the worst crimes from others?"

"He is no Christian."

"And why would he want to be when you treat him so?"

Matthys was stunned by the concept and silenced for a few seconds.

"You really believe he can be trusted? You truly believe he is one of us?"

"I know he has my back, and I have seen that he is a decent man. What more can you ask?"

"And you think you can judge what is a decent man?"

"Yes, I do. You showed me that, and don't you forget it. You showed me!"

"Then I should forgive?" Matthys asked in a strange turn of events, for he never asked Craven for such advice.

"Is that not what your bible tells you?"

Matthys sighed as he knew it was true.

"Soon we will be at the walls of Badajoz, and we will be tested like we have not been tested before. This is our last chance to break out into Spain, and we must gather all our strength, not just the strength in our bodies but in our hearts. Amyn has proven he is one of us, and deep down you know this to be true. Embrace him as a brother, for he is one."

But Matthys still looked uncomfortable and uncertain.

"What is it that truly bothers you about him?"

"He has no home. No country to return to or to fight for. A man like that can be very dangerous, for he has no allegiance."

"That is where you are wrong. He has us, and we are as much a home for him as the Salford Rifles are to most of these rejects that we lead. He fights for us because we fight for him. That is the deal, remember? We aren't here for army pay, and I pity any poor bastard who is because it isn't worth it, even when you can get your hands on it. We are here for one another, and that is why Amyn is pure of heart, and why I trust him as much as I trust you."

"That is a step too far," he protested.

"Is it? Because that man has given me every reason to put my trust in him and never a single reason not to, just like you."

Matthys looked humbled in a way he never thought he would and felt a little embarrassed.

"If none of that is worth anything, then challenge him, and

let God decide who is right. For you believe God is on the side of the better man, don't you?"

"You think he is the better man?"

"If you cannot accept him as a brother, then yes."

Matthys was horrified as he dug deep with some introspection, never imagining he would be on this side of the fence with Craven, a rogue who he sought to guide to be a better man.

"Well? Will you challenge him?"

Matthys shook his head.

"Have I been so wrong about him?"

"Yes. How many times does a man have to prove himself to get your respect? If he was an Englishman, you would never have doubted him after the first time he fought beside us."

"If I was wrong, then I have acted in a most shameful way." Matthys looked disgusted with himself.

But Craven laughed.

"How can you find this funny?"

"Because you speak like you've grievously insulted the man."

"Have I not? I have doubted the honour of a good man?"

"But it can be undone. I don't believe he even knows the extent of how you feel."

"How can he not?"

"How many times have you told me that we cannot change what has been, but we can always change our next steps?"

Matthys took a deep breath and smiled, seeing how the tables had turned.

"I came here to help you be a better man, but perhaps I

lost sight of how much work we all have to do."

Craven smiled.

"What?"

"It just amuses me that a man can hear, sense, and actually respond in a positive fashion, because most would have challenged me to a duel by now."

"I would never have gotten this far in life if that were me, for I am not so good a fighter," smirked Matthys.

"Don't sell yourself short. You've broken more than a few skulls in your time."

"I do not delight in it."

"But you know it must be done."

"I do," he admitted.

"If you want to make amends with Amyn, then you should start to treat him as a brother, as we do one another."

"I will, you have my word."

On they marched the last days to reach Badajoz. As they made camp that night, they once again found themselves surrounded by eager soldiers wanting to learn all they could from Craven before the deadly assault. They all knew there was every chance they would be killed or wounded before ever getting within bayonet reach of a Frenchman, but every soldier had to believe they had a chance to do so, and if they did, they wanted to be as best prepared for that occasion as could be. For several days the training went on with no sign of Colonel Blakeney or any other trouble until finally on the 17th of March the fortress city was in sight. Craven felt it weigh heavily on his heart. He remembered the last time they had tried to take the city from the French, how gruelling an experience was, and that fact weighed on the minds of many. They had been forced to break the siege due to a French army marching to relieve the garrison, but the truth was they were making little progress against the heavy fortifications.

Badajoz stood on an extended plain equidistant ten miles from Elvas to the West and Campo Mayor to the North; the two Portuguese castles and towns which had been such vital staging grounds for the Anglo Portuguese army and the same barrier to entry into Portugal that Badajoz was for Spain. This area was the natural crossing point for trade, communication, and for an army to march.

The Guadiana River formed the boundary between Spain and Portugal. It flowed on one side of the fortifications of Badajoz and connected with them by a bridge over its surface with two forts on its opposite banks.

The fortress was surrounded on all sides by fourteen strong bastions, which with trenches, other forts, and outworks rendered it almost impregnable. In addition to these manmade fortifications additional tributary streams flowed through and around the trenchworks, providing even more natural defences for the French forces. It was an awe-inspiring sight, but also a terrifying one as every soldier in the army knew it must be overcome, and that could only be achieved by the spilling of blood, sweat, and tears.

Tents littered the hills and flat ground all around as the Anglo Portuguese force invested Badajoz from all directions, entirely cutting off the city from French supply and communication lines. To the untrained eye it would appear that Wellington had a great advantage with near to thirty thousand troops to the French five thousand, but the French had less than half that strength at Ciudad Rodrigo and with far weaker defences managed a heroic and deadly defence.

Spring was also days away, and so French relief armies could move quickly to support the city, and that was a horrifying prospect. Although heavy rains dragged the winter out further and made it a misery for them all. Craven took up positions on a hill on the Spanish side of the river where they were given Portuguese tents, a welcome luxury in the awful weather. It was a great vantage point to view the city, just as he had chosen at Ciudad Rodrigo. There would be no more sword and bayonet training today, though. The time for practice was over, and the time for action was here.

There was no time to delay, and the men who had marched through the day were already put to work with tools within just three to four hundred yards from the town of Badajoz. Parallel trenches were dug across the open ground so that both cannons and soldiers could be brought up close to the French fortifications. Many hundreds of men laboured with shovel and pick to dig in as cannon fire rained down upon them. The men showed little care for the fire, accepting their fate. None could predict when and where a shell might land, and so they had all resigned themselves to the fact they could not change it. Men darted back and forth across open ground between the positions. Occasionally, a man would be struck. The cannon fire could do little to reduce the strength of Wellington's army, but it could certainly make their work difficult and bombard their morale in a hope of making them once again break the siege without success.

Moxy got a fire going as others went to gather as much wood as they could find. Mercifully, the rain had stopped but everything was soaked through and freezing cold. Craven and

Paget looked out across to the siege lines as they watched British soldiers carry out the worst of duties, toiling in the mud in front of French cannons. Several men scrambled from one parallel to another, and a cannonball struck one in the head, splattering his comrade with blood. It was a gory sight, but it did not even shock any of them anymore. The had fought and lived through Ciudad Rodrigo, and so they knew what to expect. They were only thankful it was not them down there in the trenches dodging cannonballs.

"Will it get better, Sir? When we go beyond Badajoz I mean?" Paget asked.

"Let us worry about overcoming this great task before we dream about what is beyond."

Yet he quickly realised that Paget needed hope there were better times ahead, as he saw the look of disappointment on the Lieutenant's face and his head slumped down onto his shoulders.

"There is nothing worse than assaulting a great fortress. If we could, we would wait here and starve them into surrender, for it is a terrible thing to have to breach those walls, but I do not need to tell you that. Yes, better times are in our future, and I can promise you that."

"Can you, Sir?" Paget mumbled.

"I can, for I can feel it. I cannot explain how, but sometimes when all things align as they should, then victory is certain. We will overcome this obstacle and march on through Spain."

"And then, Sir?"

"Then we will find the whole damned French army in Spain, and we will finally test our mettle and decide this once and for all."

"And we can win?"

"Oh, we can win all right, and I mean to."

Paget seemed to perk up as a little hope returned. None of them could stomach another retreat to Lisbon, for the Lines of Torres Vedras could not protect them again. Every soldier in the army knew that it was onward to victory or back home to England. And for many enlisted men that meant unemployment and hardship, and half pay for many officers and a miserable existence.

"How long will it take do you think, Sir? Until we can make our assault?"

"The walls are thick, and there are a great many bastions and lines of defence as you can see. We will not make an assault for a week at least, and more before we can attempt to take it all."

"Then we wait?"

"We do indeed, which is a damn sight better than being down there with those poor bastards," replied Craven as shot and shell smashed into the trenches and grape shot was unloaded at any visible troops.

"There he is, Sir, Lord Wellington!" Paget roared.

The General was indeed approaching with a dozen of his staff, including Spring and Thornhill, as well as the chief engineer Richard Fletcher who had seen them to victory at Rodrigo. That boosted Craven's faith significantly to know they had a capable engineer amongst them. Besieging such a fortress took a great deal of skill and ingenuity, something they were poorly lacking when they last took on the fortress of Badajoz.

Fletcher had been present during that fateful attempt on

Badajoz but could hardly be blamed for the lack of resources and the advancing French army which caused them to break the siege. He was also responsible for the incredible feat of engineering that was the Lines of Torres Vedras that had kept them all alive and still in the war. He was also often seen at the front lines and fighting as a soldier and not just serving as an engineer. Wellington did not even notice Craven as he took up a position on the hilltop where he could get a good look at the enemy positions, making a circuit of the town as he assessed it with all of his finest military minds.

"Good afternoon, Sir!" Paget roared to draw his attention.

Craven shook his head. No one would intentionally draw the attention of the General, not wanting to attract his scorn and bad temper or have him find some new task for them.

"Mr Paget," smiled Wellington in a friendly fashion before nodding to acknowledge Craven, "I trust the Captain is keeping you out of trouble?"

"All but the kind we have before us, Sir," admitted Paget.

"What do you say, Craven? Last time we made our intentions against San Cristobal Fort and the castle, but Fletcher would have me take the bastions of Santa Maria and Trinidad. A long chore I should say, what do you say?"

"Whatever we did last time failed, and so I would do anything but that," admitted Craven, knowing little about how to conduct a siege.

Wellington laughed as there was some good logic to it. He looked back to the mighty castle and seemingly endless tiers of defensive works.

"So be it, Fletcher, have it your way," he declared as though Craven had provided the final push, when in reality he had done no such thing.

"I suppose you would request to lead the forlorn hope and guarantee yourself a Major once more?"

"No chance, Sir."

"No?" Wellington asked in disbelief, as many an officer would jump at the chance of such an opportunity. For to lead the forlorn hope would bring much glory to one's name, and to survive would ensure promotion.

"I would not risk near certain death for a promotion."

"No?"

"A glorious death is still death, and I mean to live."

"Some would say those are the words of a coward," replied Fletcher with a cheeky smile, for he had seen what Craven was capable of and meant no insult.

"And those men would answer for themselves at the point of a sword."

"Yes, let's not have any more of that," insisted Wellington.

"Sir, you wanted fighting men. Don't be surprised when they go looking for a fight."

"Indeed, we have in the service the scum of the Earth as common soldiers."

"Better English scum than French," replied Craven.

"Quite so," smiled Wellington as he looked out to the great fortress before them and studied it once more.

"What do you say, Craven? I do not want to hear what we should not do, but what we should do."

"We have the guidance of a master engineer, and he saw us to victory before. I would trust in him."

"You hear that, Fletcher? You have the confidence of Captain Craven!" Wellington jested.

Fletcher laughed along, but they both knew it meant a lot, for he did not place his faith in any man lightly.

"It will be a great undertaking," sighed Wellington.

"But it will work," replied Fletcher confidently.

Wellington mulled over a map of the defences. He sighed as it all felt so familiar as they had been here before.

"First you must overcome Fort Picurina." He pointed to the redoubt defending the Southeastern corner of the town which stopped them from advancing on the main walls and bastions there. It was a vastly different plan to their previous attempt where they had focused all efforts on the forts North of the town across the Guadiana River. He groaned as he thought it over, though the work was already well underway anyway.

"If an engineer and a brawler both agree on how we will get into that fortress, then so be it. What more can we ask for but such confidence and faith in our chances of success?"

"If we are to do this, we must sew utter confusion, and they think they are being attacked from all sides, just as a sword feints from all angles and leaves a man dumfounded and unable to strongly defend any one part," added Craven as he finally gave it some serious consideration.

"It is all in hand," insisted Wellington, "How long until the guns can be brought up so that we might bring down the walls before us?"

"A few days, perhaps a week."

"A week?" Wellington gasped.

"We can do this quickly or we can do it correctly. We have a limited number of guns brought down by river, and they cannot be wasted. We must ensure gun emplacements are strong, and we must protect every inch that we gain. We have nearly one thousand gunners and a great many more guns than last we attempted this feat, but the enemy have made significant improvements to the defences of this place also."

"Then we know what must be done. Let it be done."

They all looked out across the Spanish walled fortress and castle in silence as they imagined what the coming days and weeks would bring. Despite the tranquillity of the hillside, the French guns continued to roar as the enemy poured fire onto the ground wherever they could see a redcoat.

"This will make or break this war," concluded Wellington.

CHAPTER 14

Craven opened his eyes quickly. The thundering sound of rain pelting his tent sounded like a volley of musketry, but he then remembered where he was, huddling inside all the blankets he owned, including his greatcoat. He sighed as he lay back. He did not want to leave the modest comforts he now enjoyed but knew that he must. Not that he had any work to do, but he needed to ensure morale remained high, as there was a lot to be asked of them all when the time came to assault the fortress. He pulled away his blankets and put on his coat, having slept in the entirety of his uniform. He was hardly fit for parade, but no man was in the conditions they marched and worked in. Out into the rains he went.

They could barely make out the walled town and castle through the heavy rain which allowed a few hundred yards of view, and yet through the bitter conditions nearly two thousand men slogged away in the mud to deepen the parallels and sheltered communication trenches. Still the French fired upon them despite the weather, making it more of a misery still.

"What an awful task." Paget watched in horror as the filthy men went about their task, which was a thankless one. For it had to be done, but it would never be considered the cause of a victory should it come, despite that work being the roots of any success.

"Be thankful you were born a gentleman, for you will never have to suffer such a day," replied Craven.

"And you, Sir?"

"Oh, I have done my fair share, though I will admit those conditions are far worse than I have had to endure."

"Even during the retreat to Corunna, Sir?"

It was a sore subject, but it was at least fading into memory now.

"Couldn't dig on the retreat, it was too damned cold," he replied with a smile, trying to make light of it, but that only reminded him of the bodies of dead soldiers and civilians alike that had perished in the cold on that fateful journey.

"Should we not at least show our faces, Sir? Might we not provide some boost to morale?"

"Why? To watch them work?"

"No, Sir, to remind them that we are in this together and that we are raring to go on the completion of their work."

Craven shrugged as it was indeed a good idea. Wellington was regularly seen amongst the troops, and he was reminded of how significant a boost that was for them all. Whilst he was merely a Captain, he had built a reputation as a fighting man. Their instruction during the march to Badajoz had also endeared him to many.

"You think I can bring their spirits up more than this rain can bring them down?"

"I don't think it can hurt, and we might get a better look at the walls with our own eyes before we make our assault." Paget sounded as if he was excited to go down there in the mud and blood under fire from the French. Craven almost felt guilty for not being as enthusiastic.

"Okay, why not?"

"You will need your sword, Sir."

"Surrounded by tens of thousands of our own soldiers, and the enemy bottled up in that fortress, and you think I need my sword?" he laughed.

"An officer should not be without his sword, for he should never know when he might need it."

"Yes, indeed," smiled Craven as he knew Paget was right. He didn't ever like to be without his sword, and yet it was more weight to carry and more cleaning to conduct after retreating to the relative dryness of their tents. He stomped back through the wet mud to gather up his weapon when he spotted the cavalry sabre General Le Marchant had given him.

"Perfect." He snatched it up, as carrying that in the rain would save his beloved Andrea Ferrara. The metal scabbard of the cavalry sabre would also weather the rains better than the leather scabbard of the infantry sword he typically wore, which would soak up any moisture and take days to dry out. He looped it into his sword belt, wearing it beneath his greatcoat to save it too from the rigours of the weather as he stepped out into the rain once more. Paget spotted the sabre scabbard immediately as the drag protruded from the tails of his coat.

"You are wearing it," he smiled.

"I am," replied Craven defensively.

"I didn't think you ever would, for I did not think it to your tastes."

"It is not, but when a great swordsman raves about the qualities of a sword, one would be a fool to not consider his opinions."

"Quite so, Sir, you might even like it."

Craven grumbled. Paget was right and he would say just the same, but he didn't much like having his own words thrown back in his face.

"Has anyone ever told you how annoying you can be?"

"Occasionally, but I do not listen to such naysayers, for what have they ever achieved?"

Craven laughed and patted Paget on the shoulder. He appreciated the humour, even if the Lieutenant did not mean it in such a way. Yet the feeling of his damn greatcoat was a reminder of how grim the conditions were in which they worked. As he looked out to the work parties slaving away to dig out the gun emplacements and parallels, he felt humbled, realising how good a lot he now had in life.

It was a far cry from traveling from village to village scraping by as a gladiator, in a time when the age of gladiators was a distant memory beyond all who were still living and a great many generations before it. He was reminded of what Colonel Blakeney had called him, a relic, and the more he thought about it, the more he realised it was true. He was indeed a relic of a bygone era, and yet he had found a way to be useful in spite of the changing times. It made him smile as he never dreamed he would have all he now did; he did not even know it was something he wanted. He adjusted his uniform and his shako to make himself as presentable as could be, finally feeling the pride in his appearance and position that Paget had since the day he buttoned his army tunic for the first time.

It did not go unnoticed by Paget who was forever fretting over his uniform and appearance. He said nothing as he did not want to insult Craven nor make him feel awkward, but it made him proud, in the way he hoped Craven felt towards him as he had developed into the soldier he was today.

"Is there something to be done?" Matthys came to join them.

"No," replied Craven.

"Then you do not need any of us?" Matthys pressed.

Craven shook his head. He did not want to be surrounded by a retinue of soldiers who were not there to do work and to dig, but to inflate his own image. Matthys was quick to catch on as he was a smart man.

"You go to the siege works?"

"Mr Paget's idea, but yes."

"Good, get a good look and remember all that you see, for that path is our future and we would walk it as best men can."

"You do not come with us?"

"The only enlisted men who should be down there are those digging."

"You would not join them?" Craven asked in surprise as Matthys was a great believer in fairness.

"Those poor soldiers suffer in the sights of the enemy, but we have done so for months on end, and don't you forget it. We have done more than enough to earn our pay ten times over."

Craven nodded in agreement. They had fought a great many battles to get where they were today. He went on with only

Paget by his side, which left him feeling quite hollow. Despite once being a stage gladiator where he fought his battles alone, he had become accustomed and quite comfortable at having a body of close friends and capable fighters by his side.

"It feels strange, does it not, Sir? To arrive after matters are under way? For we are so often ahead of the army and getting a first glance at the enemy and the battlefield before our own army reaches it."

"I suppose so but being first to a place like this is not an enviable task. Our divisions have had to encircle the city and close off all routes. It can be a dangerous task, all the while you are under the watch of the garrison of that damned fortress and five thousand Frenchmen. That is what they say is inside."

"It is not so many, is it, Sir?"

"Out in open ground, no, but in there, five hundred men could hold that fortress for weeks."

"I never imagined a modern war would be conducted against castles. I thought that was in the past. I have read that in the time of Oliver Cromwell and our Civil Wars a great many castles were slighted with ease, and yet here we are struggling to overcome them. Some of these great structures were build many hundreds of years past, and yet with all of our modern weaponry and knowhow they are still a great hardship."

"Because the defence and design of those places has not remained static either. Engineers just like our Fletcher have seen to their improvements, and even once breached, a ruinous castle is still no easy feat to overcome. The crusaders at Jerusalem are proof that."

"Why yes, Sir. I always do forget your knowledge of history," smiled Paget.

"What of it?"

"For a man who says he is not a gentleman, and appears to not pursue scholarly study, you must have studied a great deal."

"I read whenever I can. I read of battles and wars and warriors."

"You live that life, and yet still you spend your leisurely hours reading about others doing the same?"

"Not in a long time, but I used to. I didn't ever imagine I would go on to live similar tales to the men and the armies I read about. When we were gladiators, we thought of ourselves as the great heroes of old. Of Achilles and Hercules, it seems silly now."

"How so, Sir?"

"Because we were actors. We were not warriors winning great battles."

"But you are now," declared Paget proudly.

"You think they will write books about our deeds?" Craven smirked.

"Of course, they will, and if they do not, I will write them myself!"

They went on and soon neared the first defensive lines on foot. They dared not approach on horseback, not only to save the horses from the atrocious conditions, but not to attract the attention of the French gunners who would gladly take the opportunity to fire upon any officers that might be high valuable targets. Up close the conditions were even worse than they had looked from afar. Men slipped about in thick mud and struggled to dig further, yet the soldiers made the best of it as they joked and laughed amongst themselves. Craven darted across into the first parallel to get clear of the enemy guns before stopping in the shelter of the trench to get a good look at the walls before them. The walled town and castle loomed in the distance, but the redoubt of Fort Picurina was the immediate obstacle before them. It was a strong emplacement atop a hill that prevented British guns and troops from advancing to fire and attempt an assault upon the town itself.

"Formidable, isn't she?"

They turned back to see Colonel Fletcher standing over them as he oversaw the engineering works. Craven was impressed, as there was not an expectation of him being down in the mud and within range of the French guns. He could just as easily manage it all from afar at a safe distance, but then that had never been Fletcher's way. He was at the front even when he was not needed as an engineer.

"They've made some improvements, no doubt they were expecting us," smiled Craven.

"Everyone knew we would one day have to conquer this castle or die trying."

"Then they must be confident they have the strength here to stop us, Sir?" Paget inquired.

"Rumour has it that French troops are being stripped from armies across Spain. Some move to the East to assist where they continue to have success, but many more still return to France, or so I am told."

"Napoleon readies himself for another campaign?" Craven asked.

"It would seem so."

That was a terrifying prospect. For wherever Napoleon

went he was almost always successful with incredible triumphs across many years.

"Could he be coming South to face us?" Paget asked.

"There would be no reason to withdraw soldiers to France if he means to come down here himself," replied Craven.

"Indeed, the French weaken themselves across Spain and we must take every advantage of that fact, but Wellington knows it, too. That much is certain."

"Then there is hope we can be victorious in Spain?" Paget asked once more.

"Of course, but what happens when we reach France is another matter. Here we fight for people who want us to be here, but in France we will face a hostile populace and grand armies," replied Fletcher.

"And Napoleon? We will have to face Napoleon?" Paget sounded excited at the prospect.

"One day, if we can live that long." Craven watched the French guns breathe fire once again, "Get down!" he cried out as he saw a shell coming right for them.

They hunkered down into the trench and hoped for the best. The trenches provided fantastic defence to any shot or shell that landed on the ground above them, but a direct hit into the trenches could still be devastating. They watched in horror as a shell flew straight in amongst them. There was no time to move or avoid what was coming next, but to their amazement the shell burrowed deep into the wet mud and vanished from sight before exploding. The ground under their feet rumbled and mud and debris showered them, covering Craven and Paget from head to toe. A cloud of smoke and dirt began to settle as they coughed and spluttered, clearing their noses and mouths.

They found Wellington standing opposite them looking unscathed and unbothered by the near-death experience they had all just shared. Had it not been for the soft ground absorbing the shell they might all have perished.

"You might count yourselves lucky!" Wellington roared.

Though it was hard to feel that way when they were covered in wet mud and filthy water seeping down their collars and into their shirts beneath their tunics. Paget looked mortified as he was always as meticulous as an officer could be on campaign, but Fletcher began to laugh at the sight of them and how lucky they had been to survive the experience. His laughter was infectious, for even Wellington joined in and soon enough Paget could not help but find the situation funny.

"I suppose you came down here to see the French positions for yourself?" Wellington asked.

"My intention was to visit the troops and perhaps lift their spirits," admitted Craven.

Wellington knew that was not like him at all and turned to Paget, knowing he would be the reason for it, but he said nothing, as he admired their intentions.

"Well, you won't do it looking like that. Get out of those soaking uniforms and get yourselves dry and try again tomorrow."

"Tomorrow, Sir?" Paget asked.

"The works here will not end today, nor tomorrow nor the day after that. I think you have used up all your luck today, gentlemen. Do not push it any further."

"Yes, Sir." Craven was glad to leave the place as they were now freezing in their soggy clothes. Their wool greatcoats absorbed everything and felt remarkably heavy as they stumbled back towards their camp.

"That did not go as I intended it to," admitted Paget.

"No, I don't imagine it did, but it could have been a lot worse."

"I have to admit, Sir, for a man with such bad luck at cards, you certainly do have the best of luck in life."

"It wasn't luck that saved us, but this damned weather. It is hard to think so ill of it when we were all saved by the thick mud brought on by these rains."

Paget grumbled in agreement as they reached their camp. Many of the larger tents had been opened up wide and fires lit in their entrances so that the soldiers might have some hope of getting warm and dry even at the expense of being smoked. Matthys had prepared Craven's tent in such a way, perhaps to be helpful or perhaps just to make best use of a large officer's tent and the luxurious headroom. As Craven and Paget approached, many began to laugh at their appearance, but none more so than Ferreira. He burst into such coarse laughter he was nearly crying. Craven sighed but he said nothing, knowing a little laughter was good for their spirits.

"What happened to you?" Matthys took his soaking greatcoat and hung it up beside the fire for him.

"That mud saved us from a shell, so I can't complain too much about it."

"It was a close thing, and for Lord Wellington also," added Paget.

"He was there with you?"

"By chance, yes he was, and he came off rather cleaner than us," explained Craven.

"You were not gone long. It was fruitless, then?"

"Yes, but we shall try again tomorrow. That is what Wellington asked of us."

"Then he understands the importance of it. How could he not? For he is not down there in the mud for the fun of it," mused Matthys.

"I imagine he wants to keep a keen eye on the progress and to study the French positions with his own eyes," added Craven.

"It's more than that. I am willing to bet he was down there for the same reasons you were, and that is why he had asked you to try again. You mean something to this army, Craven. You are a symbol of deviance against the French. A symbol of hope."

Craven shrugged. He didn't see it himself and was just glad to warm his hands before the fire. The next day was a slow start as Craven's enthusiasm was low, for he imagined a repeat of the previous day. Eventually, he dragged himself from his bed and went outside. Mercifully, the rain had stopped, but not the French cannons that now had a better view of the poor devils digging day and night.

"Here you go, Sir!" Paget declared excitedly. He brought him a cup of coffee as if to bribe him to go on towards the front lines. He welcomed the warm beverage as all cold soldiers did.

"A better day today, Sir, I am certain of it."

They were soon on their way once again, but as they approached the engineering works, they could see just how much had changed overnight. They were stunned to see the parallels had been extended significantly. Two gun emplacements were marked out and already being dug out at a significant rate. A great deal of hard work had been carried out through the night. Work went on day and night, for time was still against Wellington. Every day that went by increased the chances of a French relief army coming to the aid of Badajoz, just as it had last time the Anglo Portuguese forces made an attempt upon the town. Not only had the siege works progressed far into the ground but also significantly closer to Fort Picurina.

"Soon the guns will be in place and the task of bringing down these walls can begin," announced Paget.

Craven nodded in agreement as that would be a welcome sight. The work was progressing at a steady pace, and yet they were all still anxious. There was so much more to be done, and this preparatory work was impressive, but it had not yet achieved any objectives.

"The French are coming! The French are coming!" a voice cried out.

Musket and rifle fire rang out sporadically as Craven rushed to see for himself. French infantry poured up the hill from the bastion of San Roque on the Southeasterly corner of the town. More than a thousand troops were sallying out of the walls in a sortie to attack the positions they had spent days working to prepare. A small body of cavalry also galloped up towards them.

"It's happened again," scowled Craven as he was reminded of the sortie at Ciudad Rodrigo.

The workforce with only shovels and picks in hand were already fleeing upon sight of the huge French force. Green jacketed riflemen of the 95th rushed forward to take well aimed shots at the advancing Frenchmen and were knocking them down, but not quickly enough to stop their advance as the enemy swarmed into the trenches.

"Don't let them take our tools!"

Fletcher drew out his sword and swung it about his head as he tried to rally the troops and gather all to him to counter charge the enemy. Yet they were disorganised, and many did not even have muskets to hand.

"We haven't even put in the guns, what damage can they do?" Craven pressed, as it seemed a suicidal thing to go directly towards the strong French force. Musket and rifle fire continued to be exchanged, and those working in the trenches had been driven five hundred yards away from the parallel where they had come to a halt, knowing the enemy would not continue on after them.

"Tools!" Fletcher shouted angrily at Craven.

"A few shovels? Get more," he snarled.

"There are no more! If we lose what we have, then we will lose days and weeks, and a relief army will be upon us!" he snapped back.

Craven's face turned to horror at the realisation of how serious this was. He unbuttoned his greatcoat and threw it down before drawing out the broad cavalry sabre gifted to him by Le Marchant.

"Come on, boys!" He swung it about his head as an excitable cavalryman would. A cry rang out as Fletcher was struck by a musket ball and went down. Craven rushed to his side, but he pushed him away, despite the pain he was suffering from.

"Go! Get our tools back!" Fletcher roared angrily.

Infantry were already advancing forward to help to their flank, but time was of the essence.

"Follow me!"

Craven rushed onward, leading a ragtag group of infantrymen, riflemen, and even many with tools they had carried away with them from the parallel and gun emplacements. A cry rang out as they ran on like an angry mob. Paget kept up with Craven's pace, keeping close by his side. He had been sensible enough to carry his pistol beneath his coat, which he now carried in his left hand and his sword in his right.

Craven only had his sabre to fight with, but he thought of Le Marchant and how fiercely he fought with the weapon he had pioneered and that gave him faith. Musket and rifle fire continued as they pressed on towards the enemy, some of whom fired back at them whilst others worked to fill in the trenches and gun emplacements. Others gathered up the British pioneer tools, with some Frenchmen carrying so many one would think they were worth their weight in gold. One took aim at Craven, but Paget shot him dead with his pistol from thirty yards, which would be an impressive feat were they standing still.

Craven was on the enemy before another shot could be fired as he leapt into a trench. He beat away a bayonet that was directed at him as he flew through the air and crashed into the man carrying it, sending them both tumbling into the mud. Craven was quick to get back to his feet but found a sabre hurtling towards his face. He parried it with his cavalry sabre as he took hold of the musket and bayonet that had been aimed at him. He ran its owner through with his own weapon before turning his attention back to the officer who now thrust at him. He moved his sabre to parry and found it was slow to get to the defence compared to what he was used to. But he lifted the hilt and pivoted the blade about at the wrist, making a great big circle with the broad tip of the blade in remarkably quick time, it descended onto the man's neck and killed him in one blow. Craven pried the blade out and looked at it with admiration. He no longer harboured any doubts towards the sword, for whatever weaknesses it had it more than made up for in other ways.

War cries echoed out as British troops poured into the trenches and lashed out relentlessly. That only fuelled Craven's anger as he stormed forward and straight for five Frenchmen. He swung his sabre about with incredible speed, letting the forward mass of the blade carry it through from one rotation into another and not fighting to try and stop it. Craven smiled as he spotted several men they had trained over the past weeks employing their new bayonet skills to supreme effect.

Craven's cold steel slashed through the French line, and soon enough many of them were climbing out of the trenches and fleeing to the safety of the walled town. 95th sharpshooters picked out men carrying any pioneer tools so that they would be dropped as the men were shot down. A great cheer rang out by the troops who had driven he French away.

"We did it, Sir! We did it!" Paget roared.

"Yes, we did," gasped Craven. He looked about to see the enemy had done little damage to the British emplacements. A great many pioneer tools lay scattered about where they had been dropped by the dead and wounded carrying them or thrown in a panic as the Frenchmen fled. Hundreds of the enemy lay dead, scattered amongst the trenches and across the open ground before them, twice as many enemy casualties as there were amongst the British side.

"A battle won with cold steel," smiled Paget as they found themselves surrounded by men who they had taught and others who in turn had been instructed by those students.

"Cold steel, indeed," concluded Craven as he marvelled at the broad curved blade he had been gifted and could not help but feel the power flowing through his hand. It moved like the wind and sliced like a cleaver.

CRAVEN'S WAR – THE FINAL CHANCE

CHAPTER 15

"How is he?" Craven asked of Major Spring as they waited beyond many tents used for the wounded. Cries rang out from those receiving treatment. He was enquiring after Colonel Fletcher who he had not seen since he was shot down during the French sortie.

"He is a lucky man. The ball struck his purse, and whilst it went no further it forced a silver dollar an inch into his thigh," sighed Spring.

"Is that not good news, Sir?" Paget was surprised at his tone.

"Yes and no. We are desperately short of engineers, and Fletcher will be confined to his bed for several weeks," lamented Spring.

"Can it be done without him?"

"Wellington is in there with him now. We must all hope for the best."

"Why, then? Why was this allowed to happen again? It happened at Rodrigo and again here?" Craven demanded angrily, referring the sortie which was so reminiscent of what happened at the previous siege.

"We planned for this, but we could not have expected more than a thousand bloody Frenchmen to come for us!" Spring snapped.

"It certainly cost them a lot more than it cost us," added Paget.

"In lives yes, but we lost valuable tools, and we almost lost the man behind the planning of the whole bloody operation," snarled Craven.

"Fletcher goes and does as he pleases, just as Wellington does, and just as you do. None of you needed to be down there in the line of fire, and yet there would be no stopping you, none of you."

Craven could not argue with that as he paced back and forth angrily.

"We did the best we could do, Sir," claimed Paget.

Craven huffed angrily, but Wellington stepped out from the tent and came to them, and that silenced him.

"He is a lucky fellow indeed, which is more than I can say for many others," admitted Wellington, who was always mortified to see their dead and wounded.

"What to do?" Spring asked.

"We will continue onwards, for that is all we can do. Fletcher's subordinates will take charge, and I will visit the Colonel every morning to pick his brilliant mind on all matters regarding this dreadful place," insisted Wellington before he turned his attention to Craven.

"Fortunate you were there, Craven, for I am told it was cold steel that won the day, and you had no small hand in it. I have heard it said that the men you trained fought with twice the strength and skill they otherwise would have."

"Skill in all things makes a man better at whatever it is he puts his mind to."

"Indeed, then drill them, Captain. It will be many days until we may make an assault, and I would have you ensure those men who do make it are as fierce and effective as those men you led today," ordered Wellington.

"Yes, Sir, and the parallels? The French may yet try another sortie."

"Our positions will be protected day and night against all eventualities. You have my word. You are no longer needed here, Craven. Nothing will stop our work short of an entire French army marching upon us," insisted Spring.

"Be careful what you wish for," smirked Craven.

"See to the training of our soldiers, Craven, and we will see to the breaches which must be made," added Wellington.

"Yes, Sir."

Craven led Paget away. "We were lucky. We could have lost far more in that sortie," whispered the Lieutenant.

"But we didn't. We are still in this fight, and if training our boys how to fight with sword and bayonet will make a difference, then that is what we will do. At least we will toil in our own mud, and not that which is in range of their guns."

Craven pointed towards the parallels and gun positions that they had fought over. They went on to find many of their closest comrades waiting for them, having rushed towards the town upon hearing of the French sortie but not arriving in enough time to take part.

"Looks like we missed all the excitement," jested Ferreira.

"Yes, but we managed," replied Craven.

"Tomorrow we might even see the guns brought up!" Paget celebrated.

But the next day came and with it brought even more miserable weather, and worse again the day after that. The parallels and the approach against the Picurina Fort were practically complete. The lines of trenches continued to expand out across the flat and lower ground. It was as if they were strong roots of a great old tree spreading out in every direction, so that they might be ready to strike against the other forts after Picurina was overcome, and there would be no further delay. The trenches almost reached further North than the town itself in a massive feat of engineering carried out by the labour of thousands of men. It was an impressive sight to behold, but nothing to celebrate, as it had not yet been used to achieve anything.

Craven continued the training of all who were willing to hear it or ordered to be there, but it was a miserable experience in the continuous deluge of water. The training party came to a halt as they watched the siege works come under such intense flooding. Any earth thrown up onto the surface was melted away as soon as it landed. Mud cast into the gabions ran off as slimy water, rendering them useless. The men in the trenches and parapets were flooded out and forced to retreat from them. To make matters worse, there was an almighty creak as the Guadiana River rose and smashed the two bridges which connected the army with the fortress of Elvas to the West, from where all their supplies and reinforcements came. The guns could not be brought up in such atrocious conditions and the siege ground to a miserable halt.

With the immense flooding came an awful stench, and day after day the rain continued to pelt the besieging army. Meanwhile, the French watched from the comforts of the walls of Badajoz and the luxuries of hard roads, functioning drainage, and solid roofs above their heads. Four days past like this, and yet still Craven conducted his exercises and trained men with sticks in the pouring rain.

Two-dozen green jacketed riflemen had come to practice, having no work to do in guarding the siege works, for the French could no sooner advance on them than the British. Craven looked down at the small sword bayonets they wore on their flanks which resembled a short and straight sabre, having a D shaped ward iron and a flat sword blade. Quite unlike the triangular socket bayonets of the regular infantry, which were never intended to be used as a weapon in their own right, only when fixed to a musket. All the riflemen carried the sword bayonet, including their Sergeants, only their officers carried sabres.

"Those swords, do you know how to use them? Have you been trained to use them?"

"We are taught to fix them to our rifles and to march with them," replied one Sergeant.

"You wear swords, but you are not trained in swordsmanship?"

"What good are they if not mounted upon a rifle?" replied another.

Craven went up to the rifleman and drew out his Baker sword bayonet. The blade was just two feet long but of fairly robust form, and the cast brass hilt balanced it well, not unlike a ship's cutlass, though smaller and with less hand protection.

"And when you do not have your rifle to hand?"

The man shrugged as if that was an impossibility.

"Many Frenchmen carry a sword not unlike this. A briquet they call it. They teach their men how to use their swords. A sword master instructs them. What will you do when you meet those Frenchmen? Will you rely on strength and courage?"

"Of course," replied the man whose sword bayonet he had taken.

"Is that how you treat your rifles? Do you take to the battlefield with no training in them, like some ill trained militia?"

The rifleman looked insulted and yet knew he could not defend himself without falling into the trap Craven had set for him.

"You weren't born to be good shots with your rifles. You were trained to be good shots, along with everything else you know about acting as a rifleman, and yet you think you can be fine swordsmen with confidence alone?"

No one said a word. They were still not convinced there was much to using their little sword bayonets, as to many they will little more than a small cudgel.

Craven went to a stack of broken staves that had not survived their many days of intensive training. He measured up several of the broken pieces to the sword bayonet in his hands until he had two lengths that roughly matched the short sword.

"Well? If you think you can fight with these, show me. Who will fight me?"

"I will," insisted the same man, as if he wanted a chance to payback the insult Craven had levelled at them. For a rifleman didn't take lightly to being called incapable and compared to the militia. Craven put down the man's sword bayonet and gave him one of the sticks, putting some distance between them.

"Any strong blow which is landed, and we stop and go again, is that clear?"

But the rifleman seemed oblivious as he came forward, bobbing back and forth as if he were a boxer. Craven lashed out with a quick strike to push the rifleman's stick aside before snapping a blow to his jaw, splitting his lip. The man looked astonished and angered, but not put off as he came forward again. He levelled a huge blow at Craven before changing levels to swing from Craven's lead leg. But for Craven it was like fighting a common ruffian with only strength and not any significant skill. He slipped the leg back and brought the stick down onto the man's head and struck smartly. The blow rattled the man, and he staggered back completed stunned, before giving out a war cry and charging in for a third time. Craven parried his blow aside and kicked his legs out from under him, whilst keeping hold of the man's tunic as he drove him down back first into the mud and presented his stick to the rifleman's chest. Applause rang out from the other riflemen as they finally respected what Craven had to offer. The Captain helped his victim up and returned his sword bayonet to him. He looked humbled and offered no further resistance.

"In a few days or weeks, we will be going up and over those walls. It won't matter how good a shot you are when you come to grips with those damned Frenchmen. I know you can shoot, for you would never be permitted to wear those green jackets if you could not, but when it comes down to a brawl in the mud and blood, and all you have left is that little sword, by

God you better know how to use it. I can show you how if you will let me."

A roar of agreement followed. They got to work, but by noon the rains had finally stopped. The bleak grey skies began to part, and they finally felt sunshine on their skin. The camp seemed to come alive as tent flaps were flung back, and an army hidden away stepped out into the sunlight. Four days of relentless torrential rain had come to an end, and their work could finally continue. The ground was still slick with mud and water settled everywhere, but with no more coming from the skies, they could finally drain the parallels and parapets. The mood of the entire army had turned with the weather, and the cries of officers echoed out all around as work parties were formed to continue the siege. Thousands of soldiers and labourers were brought up to the siege lines, and a herculean effort began to bring up the great guns.

"This is it, it is finally happening, isn't it, Sir?"

Craven nodded in agreement to Paget. For as they watched the guns be dragged into place, they knew an assault would come quickly. The redoubt of Picurina could not withstand such an onslaught as they would be able to bring upon the fortification. The work went on all day, and the sun was down before the guns were ready to fire. That did not dampen the spirits of the troops, for they knew the next day would change everything. That night the Salfords gathered around a huge fire, relieved not to be huddling in small tents from the torrential weather of the previous nights. Others joined them, including many of the men they had trained and some of the riflemen from earlier that day. Spirits were high as enthusiastic conversation filled the air. It had been a slow start to the siege, but there was a feeling amongst them all that they were back on track, and all were eager to see what the morning would bring.

"Look who has come back to us!" Moxy roared.

Craven and Paget turned about to see the Welshman approaching with an arm wrapped over Ellis, who none of them had seen since the hospital where he was recovering his wounds. He was walking on his own two feet and had his rifle slung over his back.

"You cannot have been released so soon?" Craven asked.

It had been weeks since his injuries, but they were severe indeed, and many men would spend months recovering from such wounds.

"I heard you had marched on Badajoz, and I could not let you go without me."

Craven could see he was not in perfect health. He still looked pale and weak, but also eager and stubborn, too.

"It's good to have you back, Captain," joked Craven, mocking Ellis not only for hiding his past but also using his knowledge as a former officer to receive his own room and the best of treatment when he was recovering.

It felt good to have him back, especially after Hawkshaw leaving them. It felt like the Salfords were complete once more as Craven looked about the soldiers all around him as they chatted and cheered and made merry. The morning soon came, and all were awake as they watched from afar with anticipation to see the first bombardment begin. The British and Portuguese gun batteries opened fire simultaneously, ten guns against the Picurina, and eighteen against the part of the main fortress behind it. It was a tremendous roar from the great guns, and a loud and excitable cheer followed from the troops watching from afar. The bastions of the town walls were chipped away at for a later advance, but Fort Picurina was most severely bombarded, the guns there rapidly silenced as the morning went on. The afternoon weakened the defences further as cheers followed upon every direct hit and damage inflicted.

There was no training with sword nor bayonet that day. Every soldier watched with glee as the guns did their work, but in the middle of the afternoon Wellington came before them to watch and allowed himself to be caught up in the excitement of it all. He spoke to many as he mingled with the troops, finally stopping beside Craven.

"Well done, Sir," declared Craven.

"The job is not done yet; it is not even started. Five days we have lost to the damned weather, so now we will make up for that time. I am ordering an assault on the fort tonight." He gestured towards Picurina.

Craven was stunned, for they had silenced the French guns upon the fort but otherwise the damage to the fortifications were quite minimal.

"There is no time to waste. You know that." Wellington pre-empted Craven.

Craven shrugged.

"A hard fight to take that fort."

"And a hard fight we shall give them. Under darkness, General Kempt and five hundred men will make their assault, and we will have that fort this night."

"Let us support them. My best shots may keep the heads of the enemy down, and we will provide support throughout," volunteered Craven,

Wellington was astonished.

"You said you would not risk your life in a forlorn hope?"

"And I do not. I only ask that we may assist those who do. I would have our men succeed tonight. Not for honour, nor glory or promotion, but because they need it. Look at them. They need a success."

"So be it, but you do nothing until the assault has begun. Support them but remember this is Kempt's assault."

"Yes, Sir," Craven agreed.

On and on the cannons raged all morning as they attempted to make up for lost time. The palisades of the fort were eventually damaged, including some degradation of its salient angle. It would provide some help for the assaulting troops, though it was hardly a breach that they would have hoped for. The shallow bastion clung closely to the ground and presented only a small target, its glacis facings at such an angle as they absorbed or bounced many of the cannon balls which struck it.

And there would yet be further defensive measures to stop an assault which they could not yet see. Hidden beneath the ground before the walls. There were no significant troops movements in daylight so as to not give away the plan of the night. Traditional doctrine would be to force a breach with cannon before making an assault. Doing so before this would also possess the element of surprise, just as they had used when first arrived at Ciudad Rodrigo, which seemed such a modest obstacle as to the fortress they now faced. As the sun went down, the anticipation began to climb. The troops of the Light and 3rd Divisions were assembled and brought forward for the assault. Craven assembled his best shots to support the five hundred strong assault force, just forty soldiers. He formed them up behind Kempt's force before going to report to the General himself. Kempt was an old soldier approaching fifty-years-of-age, and yet there was not a grey hair on his head, and he looked to be fit and strong. He had served with distinction across many campaigns and esteemed regiments. He looked regal, calm, and stoic.

"Captain Craven, Sir."

"Lord Wellington tells me you volunteered to provide support to our endeavour?"

"That's right, Sir."

"Not to lead it? Not to lead the forlorn hope? Not to ensure promotion?"

"I am quite sure there are men who want that far more than me. I only want to see you get up and over those walls so that tomorrow it is not the French who hold that damned fort."

"An officer who wants to fight but expects nothing in return? I can see why you are still a Captain. I envy you. For I wish I was still in your shoes. Long may you live out these days."

Craven was shocked. He had expected an abrasive reception from a General thinking he was trying to steal his moment of glory.

"Good luck to you, Sir."

"And to you, Captain."

There was no speech given. The operation was conducted calmly and quietly so as to not give any sign to the enemy that an assault was coming. They slipped into the trenches of the first parallel and began making their way to the front. They passed a great many soldiers posted to the lines who praised them as they went on until they were at the closest trenches to the Fort. They halted as they readied themselves for the final rush across open ground.

The cannons of Fort Picurina had been silenced that day, but there was still a sizeable force of French troops defending it. Thirty-foot ladders had been carried into the trenches with which to scale the fortification. It gave some inclination as to how far they might have to climb to overcome the thick walls and deep ditches. Craven checked his watch as the anticipation grew, and Paget readied his long rifle and cartridge box, feeling the pressure as he wanted to do his best. It was almost ten o'clock, the time the assault was to be launched. He took his rifle from his back in readiness to provide the covering fire he had promised. He still didn't much like firearms, but he certainly had a respect for them.

"Can we do it, Sir?" Paget whispered.

"We must. We have to make some headway soon."

"Then we will."

They watched as General Kempt climbed out of the trench and signalled for the others to join him quietly, which they did. Hundreds of troops climbed out from the muddy trenches and began to move forward. Anything which might make any noise or weigh them down had been discarded, including their greatcoats, knapsacks, and canteens. They carried only weapons and ammunition as they made the advance over the same ground the French sortie had covered. The day of fine weather had firmed up the ground somewhat which was a welcome surprise. They went on quietly as they descended upon the ominous fort, lit only by some small lanterns atop the walls. But several musket shots erupted from the same walls, and they knew the time for secrecy was over.

"This is it, Sir," declared Paget excitedly.

General Kempt pulled out a whistle from his cross belt and blew on it loudly. The shrill shriek echoed out even over the French muskets, and every soldier knew what he had to do. A deafening war cry erupted, drowning out the intensifying French musket fire as the British infantry surged forward with fixed bayonets and ladders in hand. The troops stormed on, but Craven soon took to one knee and aimed with his rifle. It was painfully reminiscent of the last time they had done the same when assaulting San Cristobal to the North of the town a year earlier, a defeat that weighed on all their minds. But he tried to put it aside as he took his first shot and struck a Frenchman in the arm who took aim at the assaulting force. Lanterns and musket fire lit up the scene well as a desperate affair went on. Moxy and Paget fired next and then Ellis, who did not fail to hit his mark.

"You've still got it," smirked Moxy as he hurried to reload.

"I was shot through the body, not in my eyes," snapped Ellis.

A furious fire of musketry was poured down onto the assaulters, killing and wounding one hundred before they had even reached the walls, but on they went. They pushed on towards the flanks in an attempt to break in at the gorge, but they soon stalled as they found a double row of palisades and a cutting. Craven fired his third shot and began to reload when he noticed the assault had stalled at the flanks. In the centre they were struggling to scramble up the ladders under an intense weight of fire as they tried to make it up the damaged salient of the fort; the only part that had suffered significant damage from the bombardment that day.

"We must make headway on the flanks, or they will never

get in!" Matthys shouted.

Craven scowled, as he knew he could not do enough with a rifle in hand. He could see General Kempt urging his troops on, but they were dropping like flies.

"On me!"

Craven left his rifle on the ground, drew out his sword, and rushed on to the right flank where they had expected the breakthrough. As he drew nearer, he could see the problem. It was far more heavily guarded by defensive structures than they could have imagined. The troops trying to climb the walls were having to drop down into a deep ditch, which the French were using to shoot them as easily as shooting rats in a barrel. A musket ball skimmed Craven's shoulder, cutting open the threads there, and he knew he had to think fast.

"Give that here!"

He ripped a ladder from the hands of two men trying to take it into the trench. He cast the thirty-foot ladder across the ditch horizontally, causing it to land at the base of the scarp, and a few feet below the parapet where the French were firing from, to create a ramp across the broad opening.

"Captain Oates, Sir!" roared one of the men who Craven had ripped the ladder away from, "What are you doing?" yelled the Captain of the 88th.

"Do you want to die up there or down in the ditch?" Craven pointed across to the French positions.

"Well, boys, who wants to live forever?"

Oates put a foot on the ladder to test it was firm before beginning his run across the rungs in a daredevil fashion, in spite of the great fall below and the enemy in front. None of them even knew if the ladders could take the weight of the men in such a way, and it sagged greatly under the Captain's weight, but on he went and soon enough was on the far side. He thrust his sword through one Frenchman and pulled him out over the parapet, tossing him into the ditch to fall amongst their own dead and wounded.

"Come on, boys!"

They quickly followed his lead as two more ladders were cast across the chasm, and fifty men rushed along them, including Craven and many of his closest comrades. With a quick glance to the centre of the fort, Craven could see that the last reserve was storming on, fresh and invigorated by the daring assault to the North and were scrambling up and over the damaged salient.

"We're in! We're in!" Craven leapt onto the parapet and hauled himself over onto it.

Troops poured across over the parapet, but he could see the enemy still rained fire down over the salient. He rushed along the walls with Paget close by his side as they cleared a path. A Captain of the 83rd led the way at the centre and managed to get onto the wall, only to be hit by a musket ball and fall back on the parapet. Craven punched one man in the face and tried to push on but could not do so quickly enough. He found himself locked in a deadly grapple with a man with musket and bayonet. The wounded Captain was about to be thrust through when a red-coated Sergeant leapt onto the parapet after him, carrying his spontoon in his hands, which was no easy feat considering the climb. The nine-foot-long broad bladed spear-like weapon was thrust home into the Captain's attacker before being pulled free. The Sergeant thrashed about the enemy using his polearm as if it were an old English quarterstaff, breaking skulls in between delivering deadly thrusts as he swept the parapet clear and saved the officer who had taken the first successful step atop it.

Musket, rifle, and pistol fire still rang out from every direction as the defenders put up a brave fight, but the British troops would not be denied, for it had cost them too much to fail now. They swarmed on up the walls with many of the wounded fighting on in spite of their injuries. A small party fled for the town whilst the remaining soldiers finally surrendered. A cheer rang out from the British troops, and it was met with a far louder cry from all those back in the trenches and beyond who celebrated their victory with great jubilation.

"Thank you," declared General Kempt, gasping for air as he got onto the parapet.

"Our work is not done yet." Craven pointed towards the fort of San Roque where a French force was marching out in an attempt to recover what they had lost. Kempt looked exhausted as he peered out over the walls to see the awful cost they had endured. More than fifty percent of the force he had attacked with were now dead or wounded, but he turned back to those who had made it onto the walls to see the resilience in their faces.

"Make ready, boys!" he cried out defiantly as he prepared to see off the French assault.

Craven took up a fallen redcoat's musket and cartridge box. He unlocked the bayonet and cast it away so that he might load more quickly and not skim his knuckles as he did so, as they took up positions on the North side of the redoubt. The sound of metal ramrods scraping up and down barrels was a welcome one as the bloodied British force prepare themselves to do to the French what they had done to them just moments before.

"Hold you fire! Fire on my command!" Kempt roared.

They were dug in amongst the ditches of the Picurina, and all fell silent. Their weapons were ready, and there was nothing more to do but wait for the command to act. A French officer cried out and they began their charge.

"Present! Fire!"

A bristling volley surged out from the ragtag survivors of the assault, many of which looked dead on their feet. A great cloud of powder smoke filled the air. Nobody reloaded as Craven drew out his sword and waited for the final assault. But as the cloud of powder smoke was swept away, they could see the French had suffered fifty dead and wounded on the devastating volley. That was more than they could stand as they now retreated back to the town. A great cheer rang out as many stood up in plain view of the enemy, waving their muskets and shakos about in triumph. Craven breathed a sigh of relief. It was over, and they were within four hundred yards of the bastions of the town walls where their guns could be drawn up and blast the breaches, which would allow a final assault on the great fortress. Now they were finally atop the fort, they could fully grasp just how important the commanding knoll was with all of the sight and advantage the ground would give as the final stages of the siege could begin.

"We did it, Sir, we did it!" Paget cried out jubilantly.

He looked about to his closest friends who had followed him into the jaws of death. They were all filthy, battered, and bloody. Their uniforms were ragged, and they had suffered a great many minor wounds, but not one amongst them had been shot through or sustained a mortal injury. He looked to the fortress ahead with a smile, for now he knew they could do it.

"Yes, we did," he declared with glee.

CRAVEN'S WAR – THE FINAL CHANCE

CHAPTER 16

The Salford Rifles watched from afar as the engineers and sappers went to work on the Picurina Fort they had fought hard to secure. The French fire upon the position was relentless, and no amount of counterfire from British and Portuguese batteries could stop it. For every French gun that was knocked out, they merely replaced it with another from their ample stores and kept up the withering fire. For four days the battle to establish Picurina as a gun position went back and forth with a great loss of life to those building the emplacements. Finally, the guns were in place, but the necessity of bringing up powder and shot cost many more lives still. The French fire was relentless and even caused two magazine explosions. Yet after it all, on the 30th of March the first batteries began their fire against the great walls of Badajoz.

As each day went by, more British and Portuguese guns were put in place and joined the bombardment. Craven and the others watched from afar. There was nothing they could do but watch and hope the fortress might crumble, but it was a well built and resilient structure. Day after day the great gun batteries smashed the walls. Finally, progress was being made as the walls began to show some signs of wear. Yet every single night the French would clear the breaches and rebuild the bastions as best they could.

The army celebrated the breaches created at the Trinidad and Santa Maria bastions on the Southeasterly part of the town walls with great joy. After a full week of bombardment, they were still looking rather strong despite the withering damage. Although there was a sense that with just a few more days they could be made practicable to an assault. Even so, a large body of water between them and the fort that was once merely a fordable stream had become a river with the enormous rainfall. All efforts were being made to breach the dam holding the water in place by engineers and sappers in boats.

More days went by as the army watched the mighty walls be smashed from morning till night. Bit by bit they were chipped away at as the two breaches grew larger and larger. They knew the time to make an assault would come soon; the anticipation and also dread was growing in equal measure. On the morning of the 4th of April Craven sprang out of his bed to find Wellington warming himself by the fire outside with Paget and Matthys.

"Morning, Sir," he mumbled.

"The army grows anxious, do they not?"

"Why yes, Sir, they want to fight or to march, but this waiting and anticipation is killing us."

"The men would rather assault those breaches than rest

idle?" he asked in amazement.

"Because they know it is coming, and they would rather know the outcome of it than fret over it each night."

Wellington nodded in agreement.

"Is this why you have come to me, Sir?"

"Yes, for an honest opinion. Most officers tell me the answer they think I want to hear, or that which they would want from their men, but what good is that? I want answers not rhetoric."

"Come with me, Sir."

They went on and Paget hurried on with them, not wanting to miss out. They moved to get a closer look at the state of the bombardment and had a fine view of the affair.

"The French guns, Sir, they are barely firing," declared Paget.

"Yes, they must be low on powder or shot, and they most likely preserve what they have remaining for the assault which they know it is coming."

"But when, Sir, when?" replied Paget excitedly.

They watched for some time when a rider came galloping up from behind with immense urgency. It was Major Thornhill, and he looked both exhausted and most desperate to say his piece.

"Well?" Wellington asked, as if expecting him.

"It's Soult. He is coming up from the South, and he has scraped together every soldier in the land."

"Where is he now?"

"He is over the Sierra Morena and is just four or five days march away."

Wellington calmly took a deep breath as he thought it

over.

"And Marmont?" Craven enquired about the other French Marshal who commanded an army which was in marching distance of them.

"No, fortunately he does not come."

"Then we are safe, for only together could they endanger us," replied Paget.

But Wellington looked uncomfortable to the suggestion.

"Is that not true, Sir?" Paget asked.

"If it were only an open battle you would be right, but whilst we conduct this siege, we are stretched thin. If Soult can force us to march to fight him, then we will pause all matters here. Yet we cannot spare too many men for that garrison will sally out once more and destroy all that we have achieved. Even in victory we would face great delays in making our assault, time in which Marmont could march on us."

Paget's face turned to an expression of horror, as he realised how dangerous a position they were in. He looked back to the staff who waited on his every word and command.

"Bring up every gun we have. Every piece. Throw everything we have at those breaches. If we cannot assault them within two days, then we are finished, and I am finished."

Nobody questioned it. They all knew how vital success was in taking Badajoz. It was the last chance of the Anglo Portuguese army, and all now hinged on a mere two days. It was stifling. On and on the cannons raged all day with such intensity as Craven had never seen before. The gunners were informed of the urgency of their work and ensured they hurled everything they had at the crumbling walls.

Yet by the evening no preparations came, and every

soldier knew the assault would not come that night. For it would be a night assault, and it would require a great deal of planning and work to prepare for in the hours before. The next day came and once more the British and Portuguese gunners pummelled the walls with their heavy guns. The army watched with anticipation until the sun was low in the sky once more, and Wellington surveyed the scene, deliberating over an assault as he looked out from the batteries at the Picurina.

Craven, Paget, and Ferreira were a little further down the wall, watching Wellington as carefully as he watched the walls, looking for any sign of a decision.

"Craven, old boy, will you help me?"

He turned about to see Fletcher struggling to get up into the gun emplacement behind them. He was still hobbling and wobbly as he supported himself on a single crutch, but it was the first time any of them had seen him out of bed since he had been shot down more than two weeks earlier. Craven hurried to help him.

"I am not sure you should be out of bed, Sir."

"No, I am sure that is true, but I must see the walls with my own eyes. I cannot advise Wellington on the best course of action from my bed, not anymore."

Wellington looked over to see what all the noise was about as everyone else was quiet, waiting for him to announce his decision. He perked up at the sight of his chief engineer and rushed to his side.

"Fletcher, at last you are up and about."

"I am, Sir," he winced as he propped himself against a wall and took out his telescope.

"Both breaches are practicable, are they not?"

Fletcher did not take his word for it and studied them himself. He looked deeply concerned and that worried them all.

"Well, what of it, man? Tell me!"

"The enemy build semi-circular inner retrenchments amongst the houses of the town beyond both breaches, cutting off the breaches entirely and establishing a second line of defence. I fear, Sir, that securing the breaches will not be as decisive as those at Rodrigo."

Wellington sighed in frustration as he could see it, too.

"The enemy have had such a long time to prepare to defend the positions beyond the breaches that it will be a most difficult battle."

"Colonel, Marshal Soult is only a few days away. We must make an assault or end it all and accept defeat."

"Give me one day, one more day, and I will make a practicable breach!"

"How? How after all these weeks do you think you can make that happen?"

"He's right," insisted Thorny who was lurking in the background.

Wellington looked stunned.

"Go on."

"Major Thornhill doesn't just work for you. He works for me also."

"Really?" Wellington asked, who wanted to be angry but was desperately looking for any good news.

"Tell him," Fletcher demanded with a smile.

"Mr Fletcher asked me to seek out any local people who might have knowledge of the walls of Badajoz, knowledge which an engineer might find useful."

"And you found it?" Wellington asked excitedly.

"I did," replied Thorny.

"There, between the forts of Santa Maria and Trinidad. The curtain wall is weak and ill constructed and ripe for a breach," added Fletcher.

"Weak enough that you might make a practicable breach in a single day?"

"If Thornhill's informants are correct, then yes, I believe so."

Wellington leant out over the parapet as the sun went down on the fortress. He could see French troops already preparing to go to work as they lost sight of them in the darkness. He was deep in thought. Time was very much against them now in a role reversal. For it was typically the besieged who suffered over time, being cut off from resupply.

"I'll give you two batteries and you go to work in the morning, but no matter your results, we make our assault tomorrow night," declared Wellington without taking his eyes from the crumbling walls.

"So, this is it, tomorrow night we are triumphant, or it is all over?" Paget asked quietly of Craven.

"I fear it is so, yes. Everything hinges on victory tomorrow night."

"Then we must do everything that we can do, even if it means scrambling through those breaches ourselves?"

"Would you have it any other way?" Craven smiled.

"I have never shied away from battle, but I would choose any other course than that. Rodrigo was terrible, and this will be worse," he lamented.

"Then let us not stay any longer, for we will get a good

look up close tomorrow," declared Ferreira.

They returned to their camp and could instantly tell the mood was different. They knew the assault was coming, that much was certain, and they could hear Marshal Soult's name being shared around.

"They know? They know Soult is coming?" Paget asked.

"The whole army knows," replied Ferreira.

"Then they know what is at stake. There will be no more idle waiting. Good, for I am sick of it," replied Craven as they joined Matthys by the fireside.

Timmerman strode into the light seemingly appearing from the shadows.

"I thought you would never come," declared Craven.

"To sit around waiting, no, but for a chance at those walls I am here."

"The worst part of it and where we are all most likely to die? That is what you show up for?"

"We are all going to die. I would at least die well."

Craven nodded in agreement and was glad to have him by their side, for Timmerman was a fierce fighter and a valuable asset to have with them.

"Do you think lesser of my brother for returning home?" Craven asked him.

"How could I? I have seen that man do the bravest of things, and I owe him my life, despite attempting to take his."

Craven was stunned to hear such compassion and consideration come from the lips of his old nemesis who he had always thought of as an ice-cold personality.

"Matthys says this war has changed me, but it has changed you, too."

"I know. We were not good men before this war. We still probably are not good men and perhaps we never will be, but we took a few paces in the right direction, and that has to count for something, doesn't it?"

"It surely must. So, then, all that we needed was a common enemy so that we might rise above our own squabbles, is that it?"

"And so the French are good for something!" Timmerman roared.

Laughter rang out from all around them. Matthys delighted in the scene as he could never have dreamt it was ever possible. It made him think about his own tendencies as he looked for Amyn who was standing alone. He thought back to the words Craven had shared with him and in this moment finally realised their roles had become reversed, at least in this matter. Craven was now the teacher. Matthys took a deep breath and swallowed his pride. He went to Amyn who turned to face him, his hand slowly creeping towards his sword as if expecting a fight. Craven noticed and watched with curiosity.

"I am not here to fight you."

Amyn did not relax immediately, for he would not be lulled into a false sense of security, just as he had on the day his people were massacred before his eyes. That day they had been promised kindness and been dealt brutality, and so he was hesitant to trust anyone. Matthys went on.

"Tomorrow we might die, any one of us, all of us perhaps, and I would not go to the grave without saying this. It is hard for me to accept that I was wrong about you, but I was. You are my brother, and I will be proud to fight alongside you tomorrow, whether death comes for us or not." He sincerely held out his hand in friendship.

Amyn looked upon it with suspicion for a moment before looking to Craven for confirmation that it was genuine. Craven did not need to say a word. The answer was in his eyes. He reached past Matthys' hand and embraced his forearm firmly.

"My brother," declared Amyn.

Craven could not have looked prouder of Matthys. Morale was high all evening. Despite the French army descending upon them and the assault planned for the next day, they were just glad to finally be doing something rather than sit about each day with the same monotony. They knew that if they could successfully carry out an assault of Badajoz, Soult would be forced to withdraw. He could not face the whole of Wellington's army which he would have to if the siege was over. Everything depended on the next day, on Fletcher's attempt at a third breach, and whatever assault would follow that evening.

The next day thousands of soldiers had gathered to watch the bombardment. Both sides knew an assault was coming, and so there was nothing to hide any longer. The French guns fired no more. They were out of shot and shell and low on powder, but they were still oblivious to Fletcher's plan.

The guns opened fire on the two breaches of Trinidad and Santa Maria just as they had for the last two weeks, further opening the breaches. But it was the two batteries allocated to Fletcher's new plan they all watched with anticipation. Nobody knew the plan, save for those closest to Wellington and the artillery crews Fletcher was personally overseeing, but it was evident to all that something was afoot. The batteries had changed their position and were yet to fire. Something different was about to happen and everyone watching on knew it.

"Here we go," declared Craven as he watched the crews go about their work.

The first volley rang out and smashed into the walls just where the Spanish informants had told them it was weak. The stonework gave in a little upon the first strikes, and it was clear to all that something was different this time. A cheer rang out as the gun crews hurried to load for a second chance at the wall. For the next two hours the guns raged and smashed the weakened wall until finally after two hours it collapsed, opening a breach as large and practicable as had been created in the other two areas in two weeks. A great cheer rang out across the Anglo Portuguese army, and now they knew the day had come. The French could not repair the damage that was done nor prepare a significant second defensive line in the few desperate hours they had before the assault would be made.

"Captain Craven!"

A young officer was calling for him.

"Lord Wellington requests your presence!"

He looked to Ferreira and Paget who he relied upon for the management of the Salford Rifles, as well as Matthys who was as much a father figure as an instructor to the whole regiment.

"Have them ready for what will come this evening. Weapons to be in good order and swords well sharpened."

None of them said a word for they knew what must be done.

"And, Matthys?"

"Yes?"

"Your contribution to this regiment is nothing short of exemplary, and it is time I acknowledged it. Find yourself another chevron and get sewing, for tonight you will go at those walls as a Sergeant Major."

"Yes, Sir," smiled Matthys.

Craven followed on after the young man who had summoned him as the Salford Rifles broke out into a wild cheer and huzzah.

Paget smiled as he watched them celebrate the promotion, for he knew just what Craven was up to. His timing was no accident. He did not just promote Matthys because he deserved it, but because of the result it had gotten by all around them. Every soldier amongst them was excitable and spurred on to go at the enemy like a pack of hungry wolves. He had brought them together and given them something to feel good about with just the same perfect timing the Captain always exhibited with a sword.

Craven was led on to a large tent where all the senior officers of the army were gathered alongside Wellington as they planned out the assault. He felt quite awkward amongst them as he was a lowly Captain, and every other man was a Colonel or above.

"Gentlemen, tonight we embark on a most audacious assault which may mark the beginning of the campaign in Spain or the end of it. Captain Craven here is not your equal, or not in the way that you might think, but he speaks his mind, and he is a terror to the enemy. Almost as much of a terror as he poses to some of the officers of this army!"

A number of them laughed, and none dared question Craven's presence even if many were uncomfortable with him being there. He had the ear of Wellington and that was worth more than many of their fortunes. They were gathered about a table with a model of the castle made mostly from wood. It was quite the sight to behold. It gave a bird's eye view of the siege which uniquely put it all into perspective. Smooth round rocks from the river had been placed to represent the various units of infantry who would make their assault, and Craven quickly noted that Wellington meant to attack on both sides of the town all at once. A wise decision, for the enemy could have little more than four thousand soldiers left to defend the great fortified town. They would have to decide where to defend most strongly very carefully, leaving some places weakly defended.

"Let me make an attempt on the castle," insisted General Picton.

The Welshman was a formidable figure. Gruff and angry much of the time with a reputation for a temper far worse than Wellington, and yet also known for his stubborn bravery and determination. The sort of man you did not want as a friend but would much appreciate as a comrade when a great enemy force was before you.

"What do you say, Craven?" Wellington asked.

"What the devil does he know about assaulting a castle?" Picton snapped.

"No less than you, I would imagine," smiled Wellington.

Picton grumbled angrily as Craven went on.

"We have ten times their number, and only one day to get it done. I say we attack everywhere we can with every single fighting man capable of holding a musket or sword."

"Yes," Picton agreed and slammed his fist down on the table in support.

"All or nothing? That is what you would have of us?" Wellington asked Craven.

"If we must. This is the final chance we have at making it into Spain. Let us not do it in half measures. Let the General attempt an attack on the castle. Let our guards in the trenches soar forward and claw their way up every single wall and through any gap they can find. Let us attack with such overwhelming force the enemy cannot be everywhere all at once, and somehow, somewhere, we will find the gap in their armour," replied Craven passionately.

"That is precisely what I intend to do. Okay, Picton, make your assault. We will strike the enemy on all sides. We will assault the breaches. We will make divisionary attacks. We will send sharpshooters to harass their men upon the walls at every turn. We will send ladders against the walls anywhere that they can be placed, and by God before morning is out, we will have this town."

A muted cheer rang out in support, but it was far from entirely confident as they knew they had a massive task ahead of them.

"And you, Craven, where will you be?" Wellington asked.

"I will be where I am needed, Sir."

Wellington smiled and nodded in agreement, as he knew Craven had a remarkable knack for doing just that.

"Gentlemen, you all know what you must do. Have your men ready and eager. To victory!"

CHAPTER 17

6th April, 1812
9.30pm

"What is taking so long?" Paget asked anxiously from the trenches. He kept checking the time.

The assault was ordered to have taken place at 7.30, late enough for the protection of darkness, but not so late that the enemy might have additional time to repair their defences and strengthen them further. The Anglo Portuguese guns had all but stopped firing, and in the distance, they could hear the French hard at work to make the assault as difficult as they could. It was a frustrating wait, but work was still ongoing to get everyone in position.

Most were silent as they waited for the order. The forlorn hope began to amass ahead of them. Brave volunteers, many of whom would die this night no matter how successful the assault. The order soon came, and they advanced into the darkness with hundreds more following on.

"Come on." Craven quietly leapt out from the trench and went onwards with his rifle in hand.

They could not see many of the assaulters for the darkness, but Craven imagined what it would look like with the same bird's eye view he had viewed the city town from as a model. He pictured the tens of thousands of troops descending on the place from all angles in a most daring mission. The forlorn hope ahead of them upped their pace. They carried their own ladders, not wanting to rely on the Portuguese troops to bring them up as they had at Rodrigo, for many had never arrived. It was an ambitious assumption to make that they might even survive to use them, but on they went with that determination.

Craven stopped more than a hundred yards short of the walls of the town and watched as the forlorn hope went on. In a few moments he heard a French soldier cry out several times as he asked who approached. When no answer came a few shots rang out. The flames of their barrels lit up the scene like a flare, and now all the enemy upon the walls could see the final assault had begun. A terrifying volley rippled out from the walls and then a second one soon after it. The forlorn hope was riddled with fire, many men dropping dead or wounded in the opening seconds. Craven and the Salfords took aim and began firing at those on the walls who attempted to fire upon their comrades. The 95th and other riflemen did the same all along the lines as the bloodied forlorn hope leapt into the ditches and began their sanguinary engagement. It was a horrifying scene to behold.

Craven kept on loading and firing as best he could, though in truth his comrades were doing a far better job. He had fired off fifteen shots when he could see no progress was being made as the desperate forlorn hope was butchered before them.

"Stay here!"

Craven rushed forwards to see it for himself and understand why they were making no progress. Great explosions rang out as he approached. Mines set in the ditches were ignited and the cry of the wounded echoed out. He reached the very edge of the bloody scene. The ditch was filled with the dead and dying, but far worse was the extent of deadly features on the ascent the Forlorn still scrambled against to make headway. The slopes of the breaches had been covered with crows feet or caltrops. Wooden beams had been hung across them with ropes and studded with nails. Wooden doors studded with long spikes hung about them, too. Neck deep water was yet another obstacle the filthy and bloodied men had to overcome, but a chevaux de fries made from cavalry sabres was the most terrifying obstacle. It was covered with the blood of those who had tried to overcome it, the bodies of several redcoats lying dead and trapped within the awful instrument.

Explosive barrels and mines continued to erupt all around the assaulting force, and volley after volley poured down upon the poor devils attempting to assault the breach in an entirely fruitless affair as they were butchered. It was a scene far more barbaric than he imagined any siege in medieval and ancient times could have been. And not one man could make use of cold steel as he had promised them, for they could not get close enough to the well-entrenched enemy.

Five hundred men had made up the forlorn hope and nearly all of them were now dead or dying. Every engineer officer who guided them was dead or wounded. Timmerman rushed up beside him, seemingly oblivious to the danger and enjoying every moment of it.

"There can be no progress made here," he soon declared after assessing the scene for just a brief few seconds.

For a moment or two there was a pause in the intensity, and Craven spotted a badly bloodied soldier of the 40th Infantry trying to get up the ladder to escape the bloodshed and seek the treatment of a doctor. For he was no good to the fight any longer. He looked so weak he was about to fall from the ladder when Craven grabbed hold of the man and hauled him up and out of the trench. His hands were badly cut, and a musket ball had gone through his canteen and lodged in his side, with further debris embedded in his knee. No one would think any lesser of him for fleeing back to their lines for he could not even stand as he crawled onwards.

"Thank you, Sir."

Craven looked back to the breach and the horrifying mound of bodies. He rushed on back to his comrades who kept up a sustained skirmish fire. The enemy could do nothing in return for they could not see them, whereas the walls of Badajoz were well lit up from fires in the trenches below where all manner of objects had been cast to make passage most difficult. Much of it was on fire. Soon enough another body of five hundred soldiers advanced to make the next attempt and scramble over the bodies of those who had come before them. Craven watched as the second wave was obliterated as badly as the first, and yet more waves came.

"It is useless, Sir. We cannot break through here!" Paget cried out mercifully, wanting it all to end. Craven remembered what he had told Wellington when asked where he would be.

Wherever I am needed.

More riflemen came to take up positions around them and did as they had been doing, making any attempt to keep the heads down of the French defenders to give the assaulters some chance of making headway. He thought back to the medieval-like scenes at the breach and that made him look up to the towering silhouette of the old castle to the Northeast.

"How would you like to take a castle, Mr Paget?"

Paget did not even know how to respond and looked back at Craven as if he had gone mad.

"Salford Rifles, on me!"

Amid the chaos they vanished into the night once again. Craven led them around to the Eastern edge where they soon caught a glimpse of the San Roque lunette, which was under assault by those who had been guarding the parallels. The modest fort had been almost entirely flattened during the artillery bombardments of the previous weeks and provided little resistance. All about them they heard the volleys of muskets and the explosions of mines. Cannons roared as grapeshot was poured into the assaulters, and in the distance all about the town was the echo of gunfire. The entire town and its surroundings became engulfed in a fog of powder smoke.

On Craven went, bypassing San Roque entirely as they passed without issue. The defenders were overrun with British and Portuguese troops until finally, they got a glimpse of the old castle perched high atop a natural perch of rock. The ancient Moorish citadel was many hundreds of years old, as old or more than many of the great old castles of England, Wales, and Scotland. It was a mighty sight to behold, but also greatly intimidating as a result. It was the tallest and most impressive defensive structure of all the town, and seemingly the last place anyone would be foolish enough to attack. And yet just as he had requested, General Picton was advancing on it, leading his boys from the front with ladders in hand. He spotted Craven as their paths converged and smiled.

"Come to do some real soldiering?"

"I'm better with a sword than a rifle, Sir. Let me at those walls and they will be yours." He ripped his sabre from its scabbard, the same broad bladed butchers blade he had used to cleave his way to success at the Picurina, and a sword quite appropriate for the brutal bloodshed all around them.

"Then come with us, and I will show you where heroes are made!" Picton cried out.

But upon saying it, he was hit in the groin by a musket ball and dropped down to one knee. "Go on, I am with you," he insisted as he hobbled on.

The slopes were steep and near vertical in parts. Cannon fire hammered the column as it advanced forward, struggling with their heavy ladders in hand. It was clear that whilst the castle was defended, it had not been prepared for an assault like the breaches had. Men from the walls above cried out in German and then English in German accents.

"They're not even French!" Picton laughed.

Musket fire rang out as the defenders fired down upon them, but after the scenes at the breach, it seemed a modest resistance, showing how poorly defended the castle was. The French troops were indeed spread thin and only concentrated in any significant numbers at the breaches, and yet they cast fireballs down over the walls so that they may see the stormers to shoot at them.

"Go on, my boy, lead them!" Picton yelled to his most senior brigadier, Kempt, who Craven had assisted in taking the Picurina Fort.

The Welshman was falling behind and struggling with the climb through the pain in his legs. The force surged against the walls and the first ladders were put up against the narrow space at the foot of the old walls. An officer led the climb up of each of the first two ladders, but neither reached the top rung, nor did the men who followed them as they were shot from it. More ladders were thrown up, but the enemy cast two away, and even took one for themselves, hoisting it up and over the walls into the castle.

"The cheek of it!" Timmerman cried out in frustration.

He took aim with his pistol to fire at those who were resisting them, but a large rock came hurtling down and glanced his head, knocking him to the ground and sending his hat tumbling away. Craven ducked down to help him up, but he quickly arose angrily and with as much strength as ever. The rock had sliced open the side of his skull and left cheek where he was bleeding profusely, but that made him angrier. He looked up to see many more rocks and debris being cast down at them. He targeted one man holding an especially large piece of stone and shot him dead with his pistol. It was a desperate affair, but far more improvised and haphazard than the terrifying feat of deadly engineering they had witnessed at the breach earlier that night.

In the distance they could hear more mines erupting and bristling musketry. It seemed to have been going on forever. Craven quickly glanced at his pocket watch to see that the battle had been raging for an hour already, and as far as he knew not a single British or Portuguese soldier had managed to enter the walls of the town. Yet on and on they made push after push against the breaches. He dreaded to think what they looked like now as the dead continued to pile up.

He looked back and saw Portuguese troops arriving to support them and another line of British infantry behind them, as the Anglo Portuguese force swarmed the walls. They placed more ladders in any spot where they could find a place to climb, and that spurred Craven on with a new sense of purpose.

"Come on, boys, give them cold steel!"

The men climbing seemed to double their pace, eager to do just that. Finally, one Private got off the top of one of the ladders but was shot dead as he landed.

"Come on!" Craven roared.

An Ensign was the next to leap onto the battlements, who was reminiscent of Paget, and in that moment showed all of the bravery of the Lieutenant. He fought desperately for a moment, shooting one man with his pistol before engaging another with his sword, but was shot down as he made his attempt. It was a heart-breaking scene as Craven imagined that could well have been Paget, but it also showed how close they were to achieving a foothold.

"On me!" a Captain cried.

To their amazement the man had found an empty embrasure where the wall was a little lower. Two more soldiers rushed up after him and began to battle with the enemy on the battlements. Kempt looked up in delight to see the success, but he himself now fell down wounded.

"Follow that man!" he cried out.

A stream of soldiers soared up the ladder as others were

placed nearby, and Craven pushed a man aside to make the climb himself. He rushed up it with such speed as though he was sprinting even as musket fire poured on from the walls above. He reached the top and leapt in with a furious expression upon his face, eager for some revenge for all it had cost them. The Captain who had secured the first foothold was assembling a force strong enough to press on, with several of the men loading and firing to keep their position secure. A body of French troops advanced on them with fixed bayonets, their barrels being empty. Craven shoved his way forward, took aim with his pistol, and shot two of them down. One cried out in German, confirming these men were Hessians, and that made Craven hate them more. They had a long history of fighting alongside the British, and so he saw these men as turncoats and traitors.

"Come on, boys, give them death!"

The small force stormed on and smashed into the Hessians with such ferocity the front rank was killed immediately to one single casualty on the British side. Craven had put his pistol back into his sash so that his hand would remain free and got in amongst them. He held one of the muskets tightly and smashed his sabre down onto another soldier's head. The hefty broad blade went straight through the man's shako and into his skull. Craven yanked the blade away and stabbed the one whose musket he was locked onto, freeing up the weapon, which he then used the butt to thrust a brutal blow into another man's jaw. It sent him tumbling over the edge to take a plunge into the castle. He fought like a man possessed and shocked even Timmerman who had just arrived to join the battle.

"Leave some for the rest of us, Craven!"

But Craven was determined not to and smashed his way through the Hessians, hacking and slashing, plunging his point into their chests and punching those who were too close with the thick ward iron. Paget, Charlie, Birback, and Matthys rushed on in to help him as more ladders were thrown up near the first, and British troops began to pour up into the castle. More ladders were still thrown up all along its length as the thinly spread defenders struggled to cover every part where British and Portuguese troops streamed into the old castle.

Amyn leapt in amongst the Hessians and fought with even more speed, ferocity, and savagery than Craven had, but Matthys no longer saw it as a bloodlust. He could see Amyn fought for them, and not for himself. More troops poured out onto the walls, and there was a groan as Picton tumbled over the walls, having recovered enough to climb the ladders and resume command.

Together he and Craven looked out towards the breaches to see fresh waves of British troops continuing to throw themselves at the deadly murder holes to no gain. They had not gained any one of the three breaches, and yet still they pushed on, wave after wave as the dead piled up.

"An awful thing, let us put an end to this," declared Picton.

No orders needed to be given. The troops swarmed on through the castle as many of the defenders fell back to the keep. Now they were inside, they could see how vast a structure it was for the small garrison to defend, far more open and spacious than most British castles. The castle also contained the powder store and food reserves. It was surely intended to be the last line of defence for which the French could fall back on, and yet it had been the first place to fall. The sound of bugles blasted out across the castle and town. The British buglers had reached the top of the wall and signalled the advance to proclaim their success. It was a most welcome sight and sound, as all who beheld it realised the hardest part was done.

Craven stormed forward with sword in hand as they rushed on towards the keep. British and Portuguese troops spread out in all directions to seek out the enemy wherever they were and sweep them from the castle. The doors to the keep had been sealed, and soldiers fired down from the fortified positions above.

"Tear it down!"

Craven pointed for two sappers carrying great big axes. They came forward and began smashing down the old wooden doors. Moxy and the others kept firing on any man who dared take them, yet a shot got through and one of the sappers fell. Craven sheathed his sabre and took up the axe.

"Give that here!" Birback snatched it from him and went at the doors like an angry giant. The other sapper soon fell, and Timmerman leapt in to take his place. The two of them went at the doors with a renewed vigour of fresh men, and not those who had struggled on for ninety minutes of hellish combat. And yet they all felt as though they had gotten off lightly as they imagined the horrors at the breaches.

The doors were soon splintered as Timmerman seemed to strike with as much ferocity as the burly Birback. Craven pushed forward and crashed through the doors only to have a bayonet thrust at him. He parried it away but not entirely, and the blade was driven into his thigh. He grabbed hold of the man and locked him in mortal combat as he drove him back, crashing his sabre down onto the man's head.

"Sir!" Paget cried out in fear for him.

Charlie leapt on after him and slashed down one who had aimed for the Lieutenant as he watched Craven pry the bayonet from his leg. "I'm okay."

Vicenta came in next like a whirlwind. She thrust one man through the heart and smashed another in the face with her pommel before running him through. The clash of steel rang out all around as the enemy were rooted out from every part of the castle. Craven staggered out from the keep. She took out a long silk handkerchief and handed it to him for the wound, which he quickly tied about his leg.

"Our work is not done, Craven!" Picton growled.

They marched on to sweep through the town to find the entrances and exits to the old castle had been bricked up in readiness to use the place for a last stand. Finally, they found a single postern that remained free to which they could exit, but as the first men stepped through it, they were greeted by the sight of a French battalion marching towards them; one of the very few reserves the French garrison must have had left at its disposal.

"We won't be stopped now. Get the men out here, now!" Picton cried.

The British infantry stormed out of the narrow gatehouse as quickly as they could and formed up. Men of many regiments gathered to form two lines, including Craven and a dozen of the Salford Rifles.

"Make ready!"

They began to load. Craven had only his pistol, having lost his rifle during the chaos and so went about loading it as quickly as he could. Vicenta had formed up with them and loaded her rifle also.

"This is the greatest day of my life," she proclaimed.

Craven looked stunned. It was one of the most bloodthirsty and horrifying of his, but she soon explained as she primed her weapon.

"Today we take back my country. Badajoz is the most powerful fortress in all of Spain, and if it can fall before us, then everything else will, too."

Craven could not understand how much it meant to her, as he had never known a time when England was occupied by a foreign power, but he could see the look of joy and relief in her face as she was close to tears at seeing what they had achieved.

"Present!"

The French were closing quickly.

"Fire!"

A volley rippled out from the force but added onto it was a score of shots from the walls behind them. Those who could not get out through the postern had taken up positions along the walls and towers above and joined in with the shooting. Craven held his fire for his pistol did not have the range for what was needed, but he knew his time would come.

"Load!"

Every soldier went about his duties with the same precision and professionalism as they showed in training, despite so many of them being badly bloodied and exhausted just like Craven. The French battalion was fifty yards away when the order to present arms came once again. This time Craven cocked both barrels of his pistol and readied to fire.

"Fire!"

A rippling volley rang out and filled the area before the castle walls with a blinding and intoxicating powder smoke.

"Load!"

They went to work, but as the smoke began to clear, they could see the Frenchmen withdrawing. It was over, and a cheer rang out as British and Portuguese troops flooded into the town. Not just from the castle but other areas where they had overcome the defences, all but the breaches, which had never been overcome in the hours of brutal fighting. Except now, when the French troops fled or laid down their arms. Craven breathed a sigh of relief. It was their last chance, indeed. For if morning had come and they were not triumphant, it was almost certainly the end of the road.

They watched as British troops poured into the streets of the town, but it was not jubilant celebrations that broke out from the Spanish inhabitants, but cries of fear and terror. The worst scenes of debauchery broke out as soldiers raped, murdered, and plundered as if it were indeed a medieval siege and the inhabitants treated as less than animals. Officers and Sergeants tried to hold the men back but to no avail, as scenes of utter chaos ensued. Fires broke out all across the town.

"These are my people. We cannot let them be raped and killed," declared Vicenta.

"Let them burn. For any true patriot left long ago, and all who remained are enemy sympathisers and agents," replied Picton unsympathetically.

Vicenta spat on the ground before him furiously before storming on to stop them herself. Paget was the first to go after her, and Craven and his closest friends followed on, including Timmerman. They went towards a grand old house where a dozen redcoats forced their way into the sounds of cries from the women inside.

"Wait!" Paget tried to stop her from getting herself hurt or in severe trouble, but she would not hear it. She soon reached one of the men who had taken hold of a local woman. She smashed him on the head with the pommel of her sword, knocking him out, but she did not slow down at all and rushed into the grand old house. She stopped as she could see rampaging redcoats taking two different paths through the house.

"Go after them!" she roared at Craven, knowing she could only go after one group. Craven did not question it even though she had no authority over him.

"These men won't be stopped. They have endured too much and now want their reward, Craven," insisted Timmerman.

Craven stopped briefly and put a stern finger on his old nemesis' chest.

"I will not stand for this, not after all the people of this land have suffered, and neither will you if you have any sense. You have seen how the Spanish treat those who wrong them. They slit their throats in the night. I can't force you to be a good man, but I expect you to not be a foolish one!"

He then rushed on towards the sounds of cries from two women and laughter from the three redcoats hauling them down the corridor.

"Sir, Sir!" Paget yelled in horror.

He was pointing to the fire that had started in the house.

"Get out of here. We will handle this!"

He did not want to see any ill deeds come to Paget, and

perhaps also wanted to save him from seeing the horrifying scenes that British soldiers were capable of in their lowest moments. Paget did not hesitate as the fire was spreading all around, and he was reminded of the horrors of the hotel in Lisbon. The irony of which was not lost on any of them, for Timmerman had been the cause of that fire. Yet this day he was by Craven's side as the building went up in flames around them. Through the broken windows they passed they could hear much of the same across the town as British soldiers ran rampant, committing the worst of crimes without mercy.

"Can you blame them after all they have suffered?" Timmerman asked.

"For killing Frenchmen? No. But for what they do to the people of Spain will never be forgotten. We must put an end to this."

"And what can we do? Just us amongst all this chaos?"

"We can do what we should do. We can be good men, better men than we ever have been in our lifetimes."

They burst through a set of open doors to find a redcoat Corporal ripping the dress open of a Spanish lady.

"Get your hands off her!" Craven shouted.

"You want the pick of 'em do you, Sir?" The lecherous Corporal took out his bayonet and placed it about her throat threateningly.

Timmerman lurched forward and launched a dagger, which landed in the man's skull, causing him to drop down dead. It was not how Craven wanted to handle it, but neither did he disagree, but the dead man's comrades did not fold at the sight of the violence. Instead, they drew their bayonets to use as daggers, but the room was filling with smoke as fire engulfed the entire building.

"Get out of here, and do not let me hear of you committing any more crimes, or you will answer to me!" Craven screamed at them.

The women retreated away from them as the men considered their options, but the roof caved in and collapsed amongst them, striking both men dead. A beam smashed Craven's head and knocked him down. He lost consciousness for a few moments to awaken and find he was being dragged across the ground by a coughing Timmerman. He was pulling him from the fires rather than save his own skin. He gathered some strength, and Timmerman helped him to his feet. They burst out through a doorway and out into the open ground, gasping for air as they collapsed down. Craven was fading in and out of consciousness, but the last thing he saw was Colonel Blakeney glaring at him with disgust and glee all at the same time.

Craven came around at first light, which he wasn't sure he would ever see. To his surprise Timmerman was still there beside him, with sword and pistol in his lap as if to watch over him and protect him from the chaos that had ensued.

"We are still alive?"

"Barely," smiled Timmerman.

"Help me up?"

They got to their feet with each other's help to realise they had escaped the burning building into a secluded little space that had gone unnoticed all night. They hobbled on and out through a small gate and into the streets where they could see Paget slumped on a wall, his head in his hands as if he had lost everything. The cries of panic and chaos had ended, and normalcy had finally returned, but Craven could only imagine how dreadful the night must have been.

"Berkeley?" Craven coughed.

Paget looked up in amazement to see his Captain still lived and rushed to embrace him. Craven winced in pain at the pressure, but Paget would not let up.

"I thought you a gonna, Sir. We all did."

"And I would have been if it was not for him." Craven gestured towards Timmerman.

"I think your brother saved me for a reason," smiled Timmerman.

"Sir, the last governor who fled to San Cristobal is surrendering as we speak."

"Then let us go and see it for ourselves."

Craven rested some of his weight on the Lieutenant and used him as a crutch. They went on towards the fort that had caused them so much grief the year before. The ceremony and surrender had already been completed as the final few hundred French troops lay down their arms. It was over. The last chance had been a success, and the last key to Spain had been taken.

"Arrest that man!"

It was Blakeney with four provosts, and he pointed towards Craven. Timmerman drew out his pistol and sword and stepped in between them.

"You dare, Sir!"

"You will not touch this man, or it will be the last thing any one of you do, and that is my promise!" Timmerman snarled.

The scene did not go unnoticed by Wellington who approached them.

"Do you see this, Sir? An officer of this army threatens

your provosts!" Blakeney cried.

"I would suggest that the Major threatens you and any man who would act on your orders, Colonel, which is something quite different," replied Wellington with suspicion of the Colonel's intentions.

"Sir, I saw these two men, Craven and Timmerman. I saw them set fire to a house and attack the women who resided there."

"Did you?"

"I did, Sir!"

"Would it be these women by chance?" Wellington gestured towards the same ladies Craven and Timmerman had saved from the disgusting Corporal.

Blakeney stuttered as he tried to understand what he was seeing.

"You, Sir, do not know what you saw. For I have heard it from the ladies themselves, and these two fine officers must be commended for their efforts and not punished."

"But, but…I…"

The whole of the Salfords came forward to join their Captain.

"But nothing, Colonel. I will hear no more on this matter, except to say this. Captain Craven, you conducted yourself with honour and much bravery. Let us once again know you as Major James Craven."

"Major Craven!" Matthys roared.

All the Salfords cried out to repeat his celebration and many more who were watching on as Wellington approached him. Blakeney faded away into the distance.

"Major Craven, Spain is open and the road to France is

open. Will you take it with me!" he roared for them all to hear.

"I will, Sir. They said this was our last chance, but it was not, was it, Sir?"

"Not whilst men like you and those who follow you keep up the battle. Up and onwards, to Major Craven!"

THE END